MW01199667

Dedication

To my family both by blood and by choice. Through life and through words we are forever bonded.

Acknowledgments

This book nor this series would be what it is if it weren't for my team. My amazing editors Angie and Maria. My awesome alpha team, Angie, Kelly, and Linda. My cover artist Robin at Wicked by Design and my awesomely creative formatter Amy. Thank you all for what you do because it helps me bring better stories to the fans, my readers, and the pack lovers who pick up each book.

Prologue

Rook

*M*y years in the Army prepared me for many things, but being a babysitter was not one of them. I had expected a higher position and a more prestigious job when I petitioned to join the South American Pride. After twenty years of hiding myself as well as the end to my military career, my decision to join a Pack or Pride was an obvious choice. Living in the mainstream human world wasn't an option for me anymore. Even though shifters came out to humans years ago, not all of us had agreed with the decision, and many of us continued to hide amongst the humans, myself included.

Now, it was time to start a new chapter in my life. I always enjoyed my time in South America whenever I had deployed there on missions, so finding a

Miranda Lynn

Pride here was a no-brainer. My tiger agreed that this was the perfect territory to settle down in. My acceptance into the South American Pride was quick, and I soon found out why. My military background had put me at the forefront of the applicants and breezed me through. I was swiftly put on the detail which guarded the Alpha Tomas' mate, Cecilia, and child, Sibby. This position gave me access to the Alpha behind the scenes, and after a few months, I started to realize he wasn't who I thought he was. By then, I was in too thick, I knew too much, and his daughter, Sibby, had stolen my heart. I would do anything to protect that little cub.

One requirement Tomas had of his Pride is that each member also had a human job. It was his way of controlling things when the Pride mates got out of hand. I didn't have much choice when he suggested I go into local law enforcement. He said it was a perfect fit, given my background and the fact his previous liaison was no longer around. I found out later the liason had been killed for a discretion against the Alpha.

For two years, I worked alongside the local officers and kept all things pertaining to our Pride out of the headlines. Add in the guard duty for Cecilia and Sibby, and my days were full. Over time, I saw the strain that being the Alpha's mate put on Cecilia and the unease with not being his only mate. Tomas had a harem of wives of all ages. One night, she came to me with a plan to get her and Sibby away from Tomas and hidden. I listened and suggested a couple of changes but was happy to assist her. If they stayed, they would surely die by Tomas' hand before Sibby came of age.

My loyalties were with Cecilia and her daughter, so I felt no remorse or fear about plotting against Tomas. One night, we ran. I had set up all of the transportation, paperwork, and new identities we would require. We found a small secluded home in the woods of Missouri. When Sibby turned four, we were attacked by a group of Tomas' Pride. I was out on a provision run when it happened and came back to a destroyed home and carnage. They had ripped Cecilia to shreds, and I couldn't find Sibby anywhere. I assumed they had taken her back to Tomas. I'd been wrong, I followed the scent of attackers to the closest town bar. I overheard two of them discussing what had happened and discovered Sibby hadn't been in the cabin. She'd run.

I tracked her to the Black Mountain Pack. I had to protect her; therefore, I requested a meeting with the Alpha and explained the situation. Jerome was a very warm and welcoming Alpha—the total opposite of Tomas—and agreed to take Sibby in and foster her. He also agreed to allow me to enter the Pack to help protect her.

I returned to the Pride I'd run from simply because Sibby, now known as Casey, asked me to. This proved an interesting ride.

Chapter 1

Rook

*E*ven with the private flights and transportation, fifteen hours was a hell of a long time to travel, but I did it without complaint. I breathed a sigh of relief when I arrived in Paraty, knowing I only had a few more miles to go to get to the central encampment of the South American Pride. Things would get interesting then. Mack and Casey had already contacted the Pride to inform them of their Alpha's death, and that I would be coming to take charge in place of Casey for now.

I leaned forward and thanked my Uber driver. Paraty, a quaint town with cobblestone roads that was hidden amongst the mountains near the coast of Brazil. It sat close enough to Rio for necessities, but far enough away that the Pride could stay hidden. Taking in a deep breath, memories rushed back to me, and I detoured through a small alley to the forest beyond. "It's now or never," I spoke to no one as I divested myself of my clothing and shifted.

Thoughts overwhelmed me as I allowed my body to take over and shift. The list of things that needed to be done prior to Casey's arrival, as well as the plans for the future of this Pride, ran through my head. First on the list was to round up the witches who had worked with her father and give them one chance to pledge their loyalty to the new Alpha. One, in particular, would be held until Casey laid down punishment.

It took just under two hours to get to the village created years ago. Not much had changed in the fifteen years I had been gone. Small huts circled the main structure used for meetings, gatherings, and Pride meals. This also housed a store for the things the Pride couldn't grow or make themselves. Up the side of the hill was the large house the Alpha built, strategic in its views. It backed into the mountain, leaving only three sides to defend. Sentinels were patrolling the forest around the village, so the ease with which I slipped past them was concerning. This would be the first test of the Pride; I needed to know where the weak links were in our defenses. I wouldn't allow Mack and Casey to visit until I was confident in its safety. Especially since a cub would be on the way soon if it wasn't already. I smiled at that thought, my large fangs hanging out as a chuffed laugh escaped my throat. Casey would make a wonderful mother, and Mack would be the best overprotective father out there.

I made it all the way to the central building before anyone realized a new shifter was in town. I climbed the steps and shifted back into my human form. Standing gloriously naked, streaked with dirt and sweat, I watched as the Pride gathered, and finally, a guard rushed toward me. "You will kneel," I growled at him. The Pride magic deep in my voice forced him to stop and do just that as a collective gasp rose from the crowd.

It was only then that I addressed those staring at me, "You should all know by now that Tomas, your Alpha, is dead, and the new Alpha has sent me in her place to handle the transition. Many of you may remember me, some of you won't, and that's okay. I want you all to spread the news of my arrival. I am calling a mandatory Pride meeting tonight at 7:00 P.M. Anyone who doesn't show without good reason, will be eliminated. A lot of changes are coming, and all of them are for the better of the Pride. You will no longer live in fear of your Alpha or the evil he ruled with. Go now and gather your Pride mates." I turned into the building in search of food and the packages I had sent before my arrival. Nudity wasn't an issue for me, but many of the Pride would pay more attention if my clothes were on.

Miranda Lynn

***

A shy young shifter approached me with a tray while I was pulling a shirt over my head. I looked at her and smiled a thank you as I took the tray. "What's your name?" I sniffed and could tell she was a cat species, but I couldn't figure out exactly which one. I could also smell her fear as she replied.

"Tamara," she stuttered as she gazed at the floor, unwilling to meet my eyes. Her breaths were shallow, and I could feel the need to flee radiating off her.

I wanted to pull her close and comfort her but instinctively knew that would be the wrong approach. "Thank you for the food, Tamara. I want you to know there is no reason to fear me. I represent your new Alpha, Casey, in every way and agree with how she wants to run this Pride going forward. First and foremost, we won't rule by fear. Please know that I do not mean to harm you for any reason as long as you are honest and willing to adapt to the new laws that will be shared this evening."

She nodded slightly in acknowledgment of what I said and asked, "Is there anything else I can get you?"

"Yes, please bring me water, a couple of bottles. I have had a long journey, and my thirst is strong." I watched as she turned to retrieve the refreshment I requested.

I sat at the closest table to enjoy the food she had brought.

Rook

"That one doesn't have a mean bone in her body. I hated the way Tomas treated her. It's a good thing he was taken out, or he would have soon broken her spirit," a familiar voice stated from behind me.

I glanced over my shoulder to find my old military buddy standing there. I stood and grabbed him in a bear hug. "Jonas, old friend. It is so good to see you and know I have at least one person on my side who I can trust. You are on my side, right?"

I studied him as he answered, "Always, brother. When word came in that Tomas had been taken out, a collective cheer went up in the barracks. It won't be easy sailing. There are still quite a few who believe in the way Tomas ran things and are not happy at all to hear a female defeated him and has now claimed the right as Alpha. There will be bloodshed before this transition is over, but I am not one of them. Sit, eat, and tell me how it went down." Jonas clapped a hand to my shoulder before joining me at the table.

Tamara returned with my waters at the same time. "Hi, Jonas, can I get you anything?" she greeted him, blushing as she asked. I stored that away to ponder about at a future time. I saw Jonas take her in as well. There was an attraction that was probably not allowed to be encouraged before Tomas' defeat. I would make sure that changed.

"No, thank you, Tamara. I am good." He smiled and winked at her.

I waited for her to leave the room before continuing my conversation. I turned back to Jonas, and after finishing off a chicken breast, began my tale. I told him everything from the beginning, starting with when I helped Casey and her mother escape to not being there when the house was attacked. I gave great detail on how I held back when I found her in Jerome's Pack and realized she didn't know who she was or who I was. The torment when she was taken and lost once again. "When she finally turned and roamed with Mack was the first time I had seen her in years, but I instantly knew it was Sibby. She didn't go by that name anymore, but she recognized me, too. That was the first ray of hope I had, and I vowed to follow, help, and protect her any way I could." I sat back, having finished my food, and chugged the last bottle of water.

"That must be when Tomas realized she was alive and where she was. We felt a ripple in the Pride bonds when she shifted, but none of us knew why. Tomas was very secretive and left with only the elite guards he had under his total control and the witch who warmed his bed on more nights than not," Jonas added.

I finished my story, giving Jonas as many details as I could remember. "I worried for a moment that Casey wouldn't come out on top, but Jerome and Mack had her back, and they took Tomas down for good. We were able to round up the rest of the Pride he had with him, but his witch did get away. Finding her is a top priority. Jerome could have easily taken the Alpha position for this Pride, but he has enough on his plate with his own Pack. He is a very forward-thinking Alpha, placing Casey as Alpha was a move even I didn't see coming, one that I think is needed. Many shifters will push back, claim she isn't the true Alpha, and no female could take that spot, but if anyone can, I think it's Casey. Wait 'til you meet her, Jonas. She is amazing and gets stronger and wiser every day. She takes everything in stride, accepts what she is, and has a head on her shoulders and a compassionate heart in her chest that will make the perfect balance as Alpha." I smiled with pride.

"Man, sounds like you have a little crush on her," Jonas teased.

"Nah, Mack would have my hide if I did. No crush, just a heart full of pride at the woman she has become. But now, we need to gather those you trust and who are willing to follow me as leader. I need those I can trust the most around me when I address the rest of the Pride."

"On it, boss. I'll gather our group and a few others that feel the same way we do and meet you back here in an hour." Jonas rose and clasped my forearm firmly before leaving.

Tamara came in to clear away the dirty plates and tray as soon as he left. I placed my hand on her arm to stop her from going. "Tamara, will you be here tonight as well?"

Still keeping her eyes lowered, she answered softly, "Yes."

"Good, I would like you to stand up here with my guards and me if you would, please."

That got her attention, and she raised her eyes to mine. "Oh no, I can't. I don't belong alongside the guards or leader. I can't, thank you, but I can't."

"Calm down, Tamara. I would like to place you in charge of those who are willing to help ensure that everyone, including the children, has enough food and water. I noticed the conditions here, and they are not acceptable to me. You are kind and have taken good care of me today. I would like you to help me take care of the rest of the Pride who choose to stay with us." I smiled encouragingly.

"Oh." She breathed. "Yes, I would like that. I will help in any way I can." She nodded sharply.

"Wonderful. Meet us back here in an hour so I can go over how this will play out." I watched as she left and then pulled out my sat phone. Cell signals didn't reach this part of the jungle. I dialed and waited for someone to pick up on the other end.

A groggy female voice greeted me, "Do you know what time it is?"

Chapter 2

Rook

"*H*ello to you, too, sunshine." I laughed

"Oh, hey, Rook, hang on a sec."

I heard rustling in the background and the chugging sound of her Keurig filling her cup. Casey was a coffee junkie. "Okay, what's up?" she asked as I heard her take a sip.

"Made it here. The conditions are not ideal but not deplorable. I have already connected with a former military mate who stayed in the Pride. I have called a Pride meeting tonight and will be setting out the ground rules you and Mack agreed on."

"Hey, you agreed, too," she interrupted.

"I know, but it needs to come from the Alpha, which is you right now. I am your voice down here, and that's it. I can help and assist behind the scenes, be your physical body and enforcer here, but it needs to be your voice I represent. Did you get the video that we talked about done?"

She heaved a sigh. "Yeah, I did. It was awkward talking to a camera. I can't tell you how many tries it took. Mack finally stepped in and helped. Where do you want me to send it?"

I gave her a secure web address to upload it too, finalized a couple more items, and then ended the call. I only had a few minutes to finish setting up, so I unpacked the other boxes I had sent. Once the projector, screen, and laptop were connected, I set up the sat link I would need to gain access to the secure network I had rigged for the Pack and Pride to communicate. I sat down and wiped the sweat from my face. The heat and humidity were torturous here. It had been so long since I'd been here, I'd forgotten that even in the evening, the smallest amount of exertion would make your whole body break out in a sweat. The air was heavy with the scents of the forest around us, an underlying earthiness to it all. I had missed that. The purity of it made me smile.

Jonas walked in as I finished up, followed by four burly shifters I didn't recognize. "Hey, Rook, I want to introduce you to some guys. These are my top men, loyal to me, and happy for the change in rule. You can trust these guys with your life. I do." He motioned to them, and they inclined their head as he introduced them, "Paulo, Paul for short, Niko, Miguel, and DJ Guys, this is Rook, he will be giving the orders from here on out."

I shook their hands in turn. "Pleasure to meet you all. As Jonas said, a new rule is in town. If he trusts you, so do I. I am going to need you as back up at tonight's meeting. I am not sure what to expect, but I know there are going to be some pissed off shifters among the group when they realize their new Alpha is a woman. My first question to all of you is, do you have a problem with that? If so, speak up now." I gave them time to think it over.

"Did she kill Tomas?" Niko questioned

"She fought him, not completely alone, but she did give the killing blow," I answered.

"Was he held down by others when she did so?" Paul asked.

"No, he wasn't, and no spells were used to incapacitate him."

"Is it true that she is Tomas' daughter?" Miguel queried.

"Yes."

I glanced at DJ for any questions.

"I have no issues. If she took him out, then she is my Alpha," DJ answered.

Paul, Niko, and Miguel nodded in agreement.

"Good because tonight, I will need you to kneel and swear your fealty to her, and in turn to me as her general in charge. Can you do that?" I stated.

They agreed in unison, "Yes."

"It's time for a change; this Pride can't survive otherwise. We are tired of living in fear and squalor. You are right, there will be anger, and some will attempt to overthrow you, challenge you, but we will stand behind you and Casey. You have the strongest shifters of the Pride standing before you. There are none equal in the Pride," Niko declared.

"Good. Now, if you can gather the benches from around the building and set them in a semi-circle facing the screen, we will be ready. Then you can gather those of the Pride who don't come on their own. If anyone runs, we will deal with them later." I turned, dismissing them to carry out their duties.

After checking that the video was loaded and ready to go, all I had to do was wait for the Pride to come. I took a deep breath and locked away the nerves that were trying to surface. This was not the time to show any weakness to a Pride in transition.

Waiting for the others to arrive, gave me time to really take a look at the building. Weather-worn and poorly patched, it made me realize that if the main building was in this poor of shape, I could only imagine what the other homes looked like. I went into the kitchen in the back only to see exposed wiring, unsafe cooking conditions, and an industrial-sized fridge which seemed to be from the sixties. There were holes in the ceiling, and when I opened the pantry, vermin ran as soon as the bright light permeated the small space. These were deplorable living conditions for the Pride and would need to be fixed immediately. I took out my notebook and made notes as I went. Casey and Jerome would both be pissed. I made a note to find out who among the Pride had the skills to repair, replace, or rebuild what was needed. I also needed to find who was in charge of the Pride financial situation. Many of the accounts, I assumed, would need to be transferred to Casey and have me added. I hated to admit it, but she would need to travel here sooner than I had hoped. First, though, I would get this meeting out of the way.

I came out of the kitchen to find the benches almost full and the low murmur of talking filling the space. Jonas nodded to me from the side of the tables, and I saw Tamara standing beside him with her head down as she wrung her hands. She was a shy one, but I felt the spirit of a leader lying beneath the surface. A little encouragement should help bring that out. I put my notepad in my back pocket and stepped forward, waiting for all eyes to find me.

"Good evening. First, I want to thank you for coming. Some of you may remember me, but many of you don't know me. I will explain that soon. The first matter I want to address is that your Alpha, Tomas, and many of his men are dead. You all probably felt the shift in Pride magic when it happened, but being out here so remotely, the news of what happened hadn't reached you yet. I am here representing your new Alpha, Casey Badeaux, mate to Malcolm Badeaux and daughter-in-law to Jerome Badeaux."

Voices rose in anger. "A female can't be Alpha!" "What the hell?" "I won't accept her." "I challenge her for Alpha."

I raised my hands for silence but was quickly ignored. This meeting would not be going as smoothly as I had hoped. I reached inside and let my tiger emerge enough to release a roar for silence. I knew my eyes were the golden glow of my cat's, but it got the attention I demanded. I left my cat just under the surface. I glanced at the five men standing guard around the room to find they were all in the same state of readiness, their animal sides showing through their transformed eyes, waiting for the signal. "We don't have time for these petty squabbles. Yes, the South American Pride is the first in history to have a female Alpha. It goes against tradition, yes. I encourage you to look around the room, though. You have the toughest of your Pride standing guard, all of them having accepted Casey as their Alpha and are willing to take down anyone who challenges that claim. Do you really want to lose your life tonight before you have even seen or heard the changes she has planned?"

I waited for the Pride to settle again before continuing, "I have a video message from your new Alpha." I used the controller to hit play on the video, and Casey's face filled the large screen.

"Why isn't she here with us now? Is she too scared to face us?" Jonas had shifted before I had completely spun around and already had the shifter who had thrown the question out pinned to the ground by his throat.

"You are the reason she didn't arrive herself. Actually, her mate and I are the reason. As much as she wants you all to accept this, we knew there would be shifters like you. Pride mates who would rebel against this change, and even though she is your Alpha, she is also still a female to be cherished and protected. So, I am here, and my friends have joined me to rid this Pride of assholes like you." I scanned the crowd, addressing everyone, "I will tell you now, we won't force you to stay. If you don't agree with this change in Pride law, if you don't want to accept this amazing, strong, forward-thinking, big-hearted shifter as your Alpha, you have one chance to leave in peace. If you choose to make a stupid choice like this ass here, we won't hesitate to take you out. This Pride oozes with evil and misguided shifters. No more! I am here to clean it up. Think now, because tonight will be your one chance to leave." I looked at Jonas. "Let him up." I focused my gaze on the asshole. "Get out, pack your things, and run. I am giving you a head start. I won't allow Jonas to follow until we are done, but remember who he is and how he got his position. He is the best tracker in this Pride and will find you wherever you go. Enjoy this moment of freedom as it will be your last."

Jonas made his way back to Tamara, but instead of shifting, he curled up at her feet, eyes aware, and started purring. Tamara didn't seem to know how to take it, yet she reached down to stroke his fur. She didn't realize it, but Jonas was already bringing her out of her shell. I tore my eyes away, pulling the projector controller from my pocket, and continued the video.

Casey's video was fairly short. She introduced Mack, Jerome, and Jaxson. The last was a surprise to me, but she explained they would all be joining her, and Jaxson had agreed to stay with the Pride to help train the medical team or to create one, whichever was needed. I watched those gathered as they watched the video. There were three more members who looked like they might be an issue. I motioned for Niko to join me and pointed them out.

"Yeah, boss, those are the three Paulo and I earmarked as troublemakers. We will follow them after the meeting to see what they do if that is okay with you."

"Good idea. Do you know where they live?" Niko nodded in affirmation. "Send Paulo to their huts now and gather any weapons they may have. I said members could go in peace, I didn't say I would arm them." Niko's eyes hazed over for a moment as he conversed with Paulo. A moment later, Paulo slipped out of the room.

I didn't have the ability to speak to the Pride members yet. When I severed ties and joined with Jerome, I lost all connection to the Pride magic that allowed mind-speak amongst them. That was another reason Casey hadn't come down herself. She, Jerome, and the coven of witches who worked with the Black Mountain Pack were trying to come up with a way to integrate some of the Pack with the Pride so we could communicate and be aware of what was going on in both worlds. We were swimming in a whole new ocean here, and the waves would be big, but nothing we couldn't handle.

Casey's video ended, and I walked back up to the front of the room. "As you can see, a lot is going to change, but it's all for the better of the Pride as well as Jerome's Pack. Now, for those who don't want to stay for the transition, you may go and pack your belongings. You have twelve hours to be out of the village. Jonas and his team will be checking the huts in the morning, and those who have left will be removed from the Pride. You will no longer have access to the Pride magic or the support of the Pride again. I suggest you find another group to join soon as rogue shifters don't fare long on their own." I paused as a few shifters stood and left. I didn't see anyone I would hate to lose. The majority of the Pride stayed.

I clapped my hands together. "Alright, we have a lot of work to do. First off, most of you know Tamara." I gestured to where she still stood with Jonas curled around her feet. "I have put her in charge of the kitchens and pantry here. She will need a couple of people to help her. If you are interested, please see her after the meeting concludes. I leave the decision of who she works with up to her. I also need anyone with carpentry, electrical, and plumbing experience to stop and see Miguel. He will be putting together a list so I can meet with you each individually and see where your talents will best be used. The most important thing is to make sure all the homes are structurally sound, and the roofs are in good condition. We will decide what is crucial after that. If any of you have questions, please let DJ know. He will put you in contact with me in order of necessity. We have a lot to do, so go get some sleep, and those of you volunteering, meet back here in the morning to get your assignments."

I watched as a few approached Tamara and Miguel to put their names on the lists. Most simply left the building, it would take time for them to come around. Having rulers who looked out for their best interest was not something many of them had ever experienced.

Rook

Paulo and Niko jogged in, and I waved them over to join me at the table. "How did it go?"

"All the weapons we found are now locked in the arsenal. It looks like four members have left already, and at least a half dozen more are packing. We will check their homes in the morning to verify. Niko is itching to hunt them." Paulo smiled.

"In time, Niko. For now, I will allow them to leave in peace. If they cause an issue or you find them simply hanging around in the forest, I'll allow you to take the matter into your own hands." I rubbed my face, the stress of the last few days hitting now that the meeting was over. "Hey, Jonas, you ready to change?".

He moved toward me and huffed. A few moments later, he joined us in human form again.

"Good. Now, I need to see the Alpha's home. I want you guys to make it your command center." I gestured to Tamara. "I would like you to join us there if there is enough room. I know I have put a target on your head by assigning you such a large task, and I plan to protect you until things settle." She went to speak, and I held up my hand. "I won't take no for an answer. Take Jonas with you and gather what you want from your home. We will meet you at the Alpha's house when you are finished."

Jonas left without another word as Niko packed up the projector and other equipment to transport. Paulo patted my shoulder as he led the way outside and up the hill to the impressive structure which had housed the previous Alpha and his harem. This house was nothing like the squalor the rest of the Pride lived in. Opulence is the first word that came to mind. Large, impressive structure. The best of materials went into the making of it. I hesitated to see what was on the inside, I had a feeling most of it would be given away or destroyed. I desired nothing that had anything to do with Tomas to be here when Casey arrived.

The house was surrounded by a tall stone fence with an ornate iron gate. The home behind the barrier was a huge two-story structure. Half-moon steps led up to the solid oak door that was engraved with something I couldn't see clearly from here. The house was a cross between an old plantation home and a castle as if Tomas put pieces of different houses together. Turrets were at the end of the building on the right and left, but columns held up a second-story balcony above the entrance. Windows lined the front of the house on both levels, including two which seemed to belong to the attic except with a mirror shimmer—one-way panes as well as bulletproof. The front door would be lined with lead as well to add another layer of protection. I could see two chimney tops from where we stood outside the gates, and I would guess, by the size of the house, at least one more would be found on the backside of the house out of sight. Examining the structure from this distance, it resembled a face, the smile missing a few teeth, making it take on an evil air.

The stone fence was covered with what is commonly known as the passion vine, heavy with its unique purple flower and ripe passion fruits. The vines would find their way into any nook and cranny and take root. As pretty as they were, a good thinning would be needed to save mortar from crumbling. The plant also ran up the side of the house. Those would need to be removed altogether to protect the house itself.

Tamara and Jonas joined us at the gates. "Tamara, do you know of any females who have a knack for decorating?" I asked her.

"Yes, my cousin loves decorating and has a very keen eye." She beamed.

"Great, will you find her tomorrow and have her see me? I would appreciate it."

"Yes, she will be excited. Thank you." Tamara had a slight bounce to her step as we headed toward the steps and the front door.

A large oak monstrosity at least ten feet tall stood before us. Heavy iron handles graced the front of the door, surrounded by carvings of panthers in all stages: slumber, prowling, grooming, snarling, and even mating. Tamara blushed when her eyes roamed over that scene, and I chuckled. "Someone should open it."

Niko pulled on the door while Paulo checked inside. "You should wait here while we make sure it's safe. We don't know who might still be here. Tomas took his men with him, but his women stayed home, and I didn't see them at the meeting," DJ instructed.

These guys were smart, I appreciated their quick action and acceptance of change.. "Very well, I'll stay here with Tamara while you sweep the house. Detain anyone you find in one room to be dealt with." I watched the five of them move together as one. They had done this before, and seeing them work, comforted me because I had chosen the right men for this job. I sat on the step and patted the cement next to me for Tamara. "It shouldn't take them long. Join me in a brief rest." She sat next to me, and we waited for the all-clear.

A rustle came from the bush to our right, followed by a small dirt-covered child in only a pair of ragged shorts, fear evident in his eyes. "Are you going to hurt us?" he asked.

Chapter 3

Rook

$\mathcal{J}$onas came out, announcing, "All clear, boss, though the women say a child is missing. We have two rooms. One with the females that Tomas kept for himself, and another with the cubs he fathered and their nannies." He stopped when he saw the child cowering at his voice. Jonas squatted down and addressed the child, "You're the one they are missing, aren't you?"

The little boy nodded.

"What's your name?" Jonas encouraged the child.

"Peter," he whispered.

"Well, Peter, my name is Jonas, and this here is Rook, and that lovely lady beside him is Tamara. Peter, we won't hurt you, and I promise you will never be hurt again." Jonas inched toward him as he spoke.

"We will when Papa gets home." Peter cried.

"Your Papa will never be coming home, Peter. He will never hurt you again. He will never lock you away. You are free from him," I said with finality. "Would you like Tamara to take you into your brothers and sisters?"

Tamara stood as I spoke and reached her hand out to Peter. "Come on, little one, let's go find everyone else and wait for Rook to come and talk to us." Peter grabbed her and clung to her pants as they walked inside.

"How bad is it, Jonas?"

Jonas sat with a heavy sigh. "It's bad, man. The women were locked in a large room down from the master bedroom, but they had no food and minimal water. They were kept naked, so none of them have a stitch of clothing on. The room still reeks of stale sex and body odor. It doesn't look like any of them have bathed since Tomas left. All the servants he had in the house abandoned it a few days after his last check-in. Then the kids, oh, Rook, he has at least a dozen cubs. They were all in a dimly lit room in the basement with one overworked nanny. The boys are in ragged shorts, and the girls are in torn and dirty shirts. They all need baths. Hell, they probably need flea baths." He rubbed his hands over his face.

"How am I going to tell Casey about this? She'll

be on the next flight down here if I do. We need to take care of it. Tomorrow, when the volunteers arrive, ask for a few females to help with the children. We will get them bathed and fed. I'll speak to the women tonight. If they have a child in that room, we will do our best to get them back together and help them. For now, let's just go inside." I stood and stretched, mentally preparing for what was to come.

The foyer was surprisingly bright, and the ceilings went the full two-story height. That was where the brightness ended, though. As if a curtain of doom floated four feet inside the door, the darkness took over. The house had a depressing feeling that weighed down on me the further in I walked. Past the pool of brightness, were two doors, one on each side of the overly wide hall.

"Formal entertaining room is on the left, and what I assume he used as his den is on the right," Jonas informed me. "I was never allowed in the house, so I can only guess at what the rooms were used for."

I continued on, having to make the choice of going up a wide set of curved stairs that could have come out of *Gone With the Wind* or straight back to another set of rooms. I turned to Jonas. "Give me the basic low-down, so I know what to expect."

"Straight back, you will find a huge dining room leading into an industrial kitchen. There is also a sunroom full of flowers and vines. Upstairs are all the bedrooms. From what I could tell, guest rooms are off the right, and the master bedroom and the rooms his harem were kept in are on the left. Straight ahead, just off the stairs, is a much narrower stairway that leads up to an attic, which has been turned into a nursery. There are no babies there now, but that's where it looks like they were kept until they were big enough to go to the basement. You'll find the basement door in the kitchen pantry, hidden well," Jonas quickly told me.

"Okay, I want to see the women first, all together. Niko will show me where they are. Jonas, you go with Tamara to the kitchens and see what kind of food can be put together to feed everyone. I want you to bring the children upstairs and into the most comfortable room, with the cushiest furniture. Let them eat and play. Paulo, see if you can find extra towels and washcloths, they'll need them soon. DJ, I need you and Miguel to stand guard at the front. No one gets in tonight." I looked at everyone standing around, and my patience snapped. "Get to it!"

As everyone scattered, I followed Niko up the stairs. I was exhausted, and the negative energy in this house was weighing down on me. I made a mental note to ask Mack to have the coven send some energy clearing crystals for the room and a massive amount of sage. It would take a truckload to rid this house of its energy, but we had the resources.

"They're in here, boss." Niko stopped.

Rook

"Thanks." I looked into Niko's eyes. "Would you come in with me? I wish I had another female here, but of guards here, you are the most approachable."

"Boss, I don't think I can, man. That room is full of broken, I can't handle broken." Niko put his hands up, waving me off.

"Please, as a request. I don't want to order you, though I will if need be. I need back up in there. I don't know what kind of emotional state these women are in."

"A'ight. I don't really have a choice, do I?" He sighed.

"Nope. Let's do this." He opened the door. This was the darkest room I had been in yet, and the stench hit my sensitive nostrils before I entered the room. How any shifter lived in that odor, I didn't know. I pulled a handkerchief out of my back pocket and held it over my nose as I let my eyes adjust. I was vulnerable during those few seconds, my cat didn't like that feeling and sprang into readiness just below my skin. I tied the handkerchief around the lower half of my face to free up both of my hands. The cloth filtered some of the stench so I could discern the scent of each female. "Niko, how many women did Jonas say were in here?"

"Five, I think." His answer was muffled by his own makeshift mask.

"Make note, he was wrong. There are seven females in this room, and possibly three more in the adjoining closet or bath, whichever that is. Get some lights on in here so I can see." Niko hit the switch on the wall, and females scattered to hide behind furniture, tables, anything they could. They watched Niko as he walked across the room to open the heavy draperies on the windows. "Open the windows while you are over there."

Niko struggled with the first window. He inspected it and announced, "Can't, boss, they are nailed shut and looks like a couple layers of caulking as well. It will take a lot to open them."

"Okay, contact Jonas and see if he can find a chisel and hammer somewhere downstairs. Those windows need to be able to open."

"NOOO! He'll kill us if you open them," one of the females closest to me whimpered.

"He can't kill you; he is no threat to you anymore." I addressed all of them, "Tomas Alejandro is no longer your Alpha. He is dead." Wails erupted in the room, in joy or sadness, I didn't know. "I will not hurt you, but I do need to ask you some questions. If you could all come out and sit around the couches, please. I have a team member preparing food and drinks for you. Something light as we weren't sure when you ate last."

"Maybe a week ago," a petite blonde answered, her voice hoarse from lack of use.

A knock sounded behind me. Jonas walked in the room with a tray filled with a large pot and freshly sliced bread. Tamara followed him with another tray holding mugs. "I figured a broth and bread would be best to start with since I didn't know when they ate last. From what I just heard, I chose right." Tamara let Jonas fill the mugs and hand them out with a piece of bread to each of the women and came to me. In a lowered voice, she stated, "Jonas and I brought the children up, but the Nanny they have is old and can't keep up with them all. We need more help." No matter how low her voice, everyone in the room heard her. One of the youngest looking females perked up.

I pointed to her. "What is your name?"

She swallowed her bite of bread before answering, "Jasmine, my little brother is with the cubs downstairs. I can help if you want." She seemed to be the least broken of the bunch.

"I would like to speak with you first. Join me in the hall." I left Niko to monitor the room and waited for the young shifter to join me. She stood before me naked. "Do you have clothes anywhere in the house?"

She nodded as she finished the last of her bread. "Yes, in the room next door, he kept spare clothes. We only wore them when he was entertaining visitors, and sometimes not even then."

"Jonas, see if you can get into that room and find a dress to cover Jasmine with." I gazed at her again. "How long have you been in that room?"

"This time, or since he moved me from the

basement?" she asked in return.

"Both"

"It's been over a week since anyone has come into the room, but I have been in there about six months, I think. Time moves differently in that room. We don't know if it's day or night or what day of the week or month it is. We aren't allowed clocks, or TV, or anything that can connect us to anything except him." She put the dress on that Jonas brought, it was baggy but covered her adequately.

"Why did he keep you all there?"

"We were his. Any female shifter of cub bearing age was brought to him and added to his collection. He called us his wives, though we never married, and he only completed the mating ritual years ago with one female–before I was born. She has become a legend among the women because she was the only one that ever got away. Many of us don't believe she is real, though, just a tale to keep hope up." She spoke as if this was the normal way a Pride or Pack was run.

"She's real, and it's her daughter that defeated Tomas, and in turn, has become your new Alpha," I told her.

"A female Alpha, yeah, right," she scoffed.

"It's true, declared by the strongest Alpha in the U.S. She defeated Tomas, inflicted the death blow."

"Then why are you here and not she?" Jasmine challenged.

Rook

"You're a smart girl, and that's a good question. Walk with me to the cubs, and I'll try to explain. I am here in her stead as her general. I came to make sure things were safe before she and her mate arrived. Her story is unique and hers to tell, but she is strong, compassionate, and ready to take the shifters to the next level of survival. She is learning all she can from the Black Mountain Pack Alpha before she arrives as well. So, until she travels here, I will do what I can to turn this Pride into what it should be." I paused to gauge her reaction. Her eyebrows rose for a moment before settling over eyes full of curiosity and a spark of hope. Her radiant smile took my next breath. Refocusing on the conversation at hand, hoping my voice didn't betray my mounting attraction. "Could you accept a female Alpha?"

"I think anyone who can handle the job and proves themselves should have it. If it's a female, then more power to her. I wouldn't want that responsibility myself, but could I accept a female? Yes."

I could tell by the noise coming from behind the door, we had arrived at the room with the cubs. Jasmine's face lit up with a smile.

"They are giving Nanny a hard time. Stink pots is what they all are." She looked at me. "Any other questions?"

"Yes, how old are you?" That wasn't the question I had intended to come out, but my cat wanted to know as well. She jumped and twitched slightly before catching herself. My question had caught her off guard. Her shoulders straightened, and her scent was stronger away from that filthy room. He and I were both interested in knowing more about this female. She intrigued me. There was strength hidden in her that flitted to the surface when she spoke. Her eyes changed when she talked about the cubs; love and tenderness with a bit of amusement swirled in their depths. A fierce protective air to her stance warned anyone that she would give all she was to safeguard them.

"I'm twenty-eight." She paused and continued seeing the confusion on my face. "Tomas kept me in the basement longer than most because I have a way with the children. I was the only one for a few years that could keep them calm and quiet when needed. About six months ago, he began to notice me as more than a babysitter, so he moved me upstairs to the harem room." She took a deep breath, "I guess I should count myself lucky that he was greedy and a jealous type. I wasn't shared with anyone, and he only gave me his attentions when my cycle came around." A broken laugh escaped her lips. "I am also thankful that he was drunk more times than not and didn't know the first thing about when a female is actually fertile."

Rage filled my veins at the injustice and how detached she sounded as she spoke. I reached out and squeezed her shoulder, unknowing how else to ease the pain she felt. "Thank you." I met her eyes, putting my appreciation and feelings into my gaze. Or I hoped I was. "Please, go on in. Tamara will join you shortly with more food for the cubs, and Jonas will be bringing in washtubs and clean clothes if he can find them." I gave a smile of encouragement, knowing that giving her this, something she could physically do, wouldn't heal the pain but might help in other ways.

She laughed. "Bathe them? That will be a sight to see. I hope there isn't anything in this room you want to keep."

"Nope, they can destroy it for all I care." I smiled back as I watched her enter.

"Hey, rug rats, leave Nanny alone. You know she's too old for you to rough house with." The rest of her words trailed off as the heavy door closed after her.

I breathed in deeply, taking in the small whiff of her true scent that I found. I locked it away to examine closer later. I climbed the stairs again to rejoin Niko, meeting Tamara and Jonas on the way with a smile as we passed. I found the women clothed and calm when I returned. "Hello again, ladies. I am sure you have questions, as do I. Will you permit me to sit and talk with you?" I allowed my gaze to drift around the room, trying to meet each one's eyes to reassure them I meant no harm. I pulled a large ottoman in front of them and sat. Niko moved to stand behind me and to my left.

"Let me introduce myself properly. My name is Rook, and I was a part of this Pride many years ago. I left for reasons that will be explained in time and have returned as the general for your new Alpha. Behind me is Niko, many of you probably know him. He is one of four I trust to help me usher in a new era for this Pride, starting with getting you and your cubs out of this house and back into the Pride." A glimmer of hope entered a few eyes.

I spent the rest of the night with those women., learning about them and their stories. Each one broke my heart more and made me wish Tomas was still alive just so I could kill him all over again. The degradation he put these women through was inexcusable. I realized many of these women would need professional help before they could ever truly heal. Some of the most broken had three or four cubs in the room below, and they didn't even know them. The cubs were taken from them upon birth and put on the third floor in a nursery where they were cared for by Alpha approved nannies and wet nurses. These cubs didn't even know their true moms. I needed to let Casey know that bringing a therapist would be beneficial. Maybe more than one.

The most recent additions to the group weren't as broken, though they hadn't conceived yet. Tomas had taken all breeding age women for himself. All the cubs were brothers and sisters. That could become an issue as they grew, but for now, they were okay. By doing this, he controlled the population and those in the Pride. He used the women as rewards for those most loyal to him, forcing them to perform sexual favors for his elite guardsmen or visiting members of packs he wanted to align himself with. The women and their stories enraged the man and tiger, both of us wishing he were still alive so we could rip him limb from limb. The sun began to crest over the treetops as I finally ended the session. I sent the women to rest in the guest rooms of the house and took myself to the kitchen for a cup of coffee and a chat with Tamara and the men. Niko left the room sometime earlier in the night when he confirmed there was no threat.

Everyone congregated in the kitchen around a fresh pot of coffee. I poured myself a mug and joined them. "We have a long road ahead of us, what is up first today?"

"We are going to need a doctor to check out the children, and someone needs to run to town for supplies. I think you need to fill Casey in on what we have learned," Jonas offered.

"Mack's not going to be happy."

Chapter 4

Jasmine

*W*e all felt the shift in Pride magic when it happened, but we couldn't truly trust it. Tomas had pulled stunts before to test us, to see how we would react. We couldn't be sure if what we felt was real or just a spell his witch created to try us once again. Rook confirmed that what we felt was indeed the truth, and a sense of relief washed over me. I didn't have to worry if today would be the day he chose me to be his mate for the day, or if he would force me to shift and let his men chase me, giving the winner free rein. I was free. I worried about the others, though. Some in the harem had been here for years and knew nothing else. A few of them would recover with help and possibly live happy lives, but some, I feared, wouldn't take the transition well.

My initial reaction to Rook bothered me as well. I felt an immediate attraction, and my cat paced in the cage I kept her locked away in. She was pissed at me, but I shoved her to the back. Even if she wanted him, and honestly, I did too, I was too damaged to be considered for a mate.

I looked over the room of cubs and worried about them the most. None of them knew who their mother was, and now, their father was dead, leaving them orphans. I was their protector, and I didn't know what Rook and the new Alpha had planned, but I would fight for these kids with my life. They would be raised in this Pride. I knew they couldn't find mates here since they were of the same bloodline; however, that would be something to deal with in the future. For now, I needed to make sure their bellies were full and get them clean.

"Hey, did you guys hear me?" I clapped my hands. Most of them, except for the youngest two, stilled and looked at me. I raised my voice a notch. "Settle down and listen." I waited, but they still ignored me. I focused deep to pull authority from my animal side. For my self-preservation, I didn't let her out often. The less I rebelled, the better things were, that lesson, I learned young. I opened my eyes, and I knew that they had changed shape; I was staring at the cubs through cat eyes. "I said, listen." My voice reverberated through the room charged with a power I had never heard before. Whatever it was, made everyone stop and settle. I took a deep breath and forced my animal back to her resting place.

"Now, here is what we are going to do. Ms. Tamara will be bringing us more food and drinks. We will sit like good little boys and girls, we will use our table manners, and we will be nice to each other. Then, when you are done, Mr. Jonas will be bringing in two baths, one for the boys and one for the girls." I held my hand up at the sounds of whining. "I won't hear it. You are all filthy and probably covered in fleas, and you smell horrible. Now, you have two choices, you can either wash yourself, or one of us will wash you. Trust me, you don't want me to have to wash you, so do a good job. For the youngest ones, of course, we will help with your baths." I scanned the eyes that were watching me, ensuring I still had their attention. "Once we all get full and clean, we may be able to convince Miss Tamara to stay and tell us a story. Would you all like that?"

A resounding "yeah" filled the room. Their little happy, eager voices made me smile. They had no clue what they had been put through because they didn't know any other way of life. I couldn't wait to get permission to take them outside and show them how to really play. The door behind me opened, jarring me from my daydream of playing with the kids in the yard. Tamara and Jonas came in with trays full of sandwiches, apples, bananas, and bottles of water. Miguel followed with a large folding table. Niko and DJ brought in chairs and left them to be put around the table when it was assembled. It took only moments to put it all together and get the cubs seated.

I smiled a thank you to Niko and Miguel as they left the room. Jonas came to stand beside me and watch. "Hungry little devils, aren't they?" He chuckled.

"Yup, and the food will be gone in moments. Now would be a good time to bring the tubs in, while they are occupied. I have threatened and bribed them, but we will still have a challenge on our hands to get them clean."

"Our hands?" Jonas cocked an eyebrow.

I looked at the floor, realizing what I had said, hoping I hadn't angered him. Jonas had never been one of the inner circle allowed access to the harem, but I still didn't know what kind of man or shifter he was. My voice wobbled when I replied, "I'm sorry, I didn't mean to say us. I didn't mean to order you. I meant to ask if you would help. It would help the cubs if they had a male assist them, show them how to wash properly, but if you don't want to, it's okay. I can do it." I held my breath and closed my eyes, waiting for a response.

"Jonas, it won't hurt for you to help. Those boys need all the male connection they can get right now," Tamara agreed.

Rook

I peeked up at him. Jonas' eyes softened as he gazed down at Tamara. She was too busy watching the cubs eat to notice. "You have a good point, Tam." He looked back at me. "Okay, I'll help the little buggers. Let me go inform Rook of the plans in case he needs me in the next couple of hours." He left to finish his tasks.

Niko and Jonas brought in the tubs a few minutes later. Half the cubs were already finished with their supper and getting fidgety. Paulo followed them with two huge containers of steaming water. As they worked to get things set up, my thoughts drifted upstairs to Rook and what he was learning in the harem. Seeing Niko down here was an indication Rook felt comfortable sitting and talking with them. I knew those women well, a few would talk, and the stories they would tell were horrible. My heart skipped a beat, thinking about how those stories would affect Rook. I hoped that learning what kind of a Pride he had walked into would scare him away.

I couldn't relive the horror and was a relief that I was needed with the cubs. Rook made me feel things I never thought possible. Once he noticed my developed body, I had become a favorite of Tomas'. That was bad enough, but to admit I had offered myself up when he started eyeing some of the other cubs I had helped raise… That I learned to lock away the fear, the memories as soon as it happened… That I even locked away my cat, not allowing her to protect me because it only made things worse… My cat hadn't run in years, she only came out when Tomas forced her. We had been ruled by fear for so many years, none of us knew any other way of life. I looked forward to the change for the others, to the hope that a healthy life could be found. For me, that hope left long ago, and I simply wanted the ability to focus on the cubs until I knew they were safe and in good hands. The idea of having a mate left me years ago until I met Rook. I always thought no one would want a used up, damaged shifter like me. His heated glances, soft touch, and above all, his scent indicated otherwise. I didn't even know if I could let anyone close enough, but with Rook, I wanted to try.

I focused my attention back on the cubs and the task at hand. It took us a little over two hours, but they were all clean, dry, and in fresh clothes. We had rounded up all the blankets we could find and had them snuggled on the couches and the floor in front of the fireplace. It was too warm for a fire this time of year, but the cubs didn't care. I tucked the last one in and stood. "Okay, everyone, who wants a story?"

Tiny voices answered me.

"I do!"

"We do."

"Oh, please."

I laughed and turned toward Tamara, who had settled into the wingback chair facing the couch and mound of cubs in blankets. "Alright, you guys, but you have to be quiet and still." She waited until the fidgeting had stopped before she began, "Shall I tell you how we became who we are?" Little heads nodded in answer.

I snuck out the door as Tamara's melodic voice began the tale. The cubs would be asleep before she got halfway through. Quietly, I closed the door behind me and headed up the stairs, needing to check on the other women. A small part of me yearned to observe Rook, too. A tiny sliver allowed the attraction I felt to blossom. Secretly, of course, because I knew he'd never desire someone as screwed up as me. I stopped a few steps from the door and listened. Even though I had been a part of the harem for six months, I hadn't heard the individual women's stories. I leaned against the wall, sliding down into a sitting position and wrapping my arms around my knees. I sat that way for the next couple hours listening to tale after tale while tears fell down my face. I silently cried for every woman and the hell Tomas had put them through. My mind raced with ideas on how to help them.

I was lost in thought until I heard Rook begin to move. I recognized him by the slight differences in sounds as he moved. The steps were a bit heavier and purposeful, his scent became stronger, and the anger he radiated preceded him through the door. I stood as quietly as possible and ran around the corner to the back stairs that led to the kitchens, trying not to get caught listening in. A deep-seated instinct drove me to provide for him. Enough coffee and food to sustain him for the day. I quickly made my way down the stairs to prepare what I thought he might need.

I found Niko, Paulo, and DJ sitting at the table. Tamara was at the stove, stirring something in a pot and flipping pancakes in a pan. Miguel and Rook were the only two absent. A pot of coffee sat on a trivet on the table while another percolated in the coffeemaker. I guess everyone had the same idea I did.

"Have a seat, Jasmine. You look as tired as the rest of us feel." Niko motioned to the seat next to him.

"I'm okay. I need to get coffee and food ready, Rook is on his way down." I kept my eyes to the floor and poured a mug of coffee for Rook as he walked in. I handed it to him as he passed by and sat across the table from where I stood. I stole a glance at him. He nodded at me as he sat and encircled the mug with both hands. I could read the exhaustion and pain in his face and wished I could do something to wipe it away. Instead, I piled a plate high with food and set it in front of him.

Rook glanced around the table. "We have a long road ahead of us. What is up first today? Where's Miguel?"

"He is doing a perimeter sweep. We have been taking turns every half hour throughout the night. Shifters have been arriving at the gates since about 1:00

48

A.M., but none have attempted to climb the walls. They are just waiting there. You will probably have to address them before we head back down to the meeting hall," Jonas informed him. "We are going to need a doctor to check out the children, and someone needs to run to town for supplies. I think you need to call Casey and fill her in before we do anything else," Jonas offered.

"Mack won't be happy," Rook stated as he took another sip of coffee.

"Nobody is going anywhere 'til you eat," Tamara declared as she placed plates with mounds of food on the table for everyone else. "Jasmine, sit and eat. You need food, too."

"No, I'm fine." I moved to stand at the back of the room.

Rook looked at me then. "No, sit and eat. You have helped so much, I know you are as exhausted as the rest of us." He motioned to the seat across from him.

I sat, and Tamara put a plate in front of me and a cup of coffee. I picked at my food. I had never been allowed to eat with others, and I felt very self-conscious doing so. I wanted to melt into the background, out of sight, away from everyone's eyes.

"I'll call Casey after breakfast." Rook addressed the others at the table and dug into his food.

I was fidgety, needing to do something. I stood

and refilled everyone's mugs and took the empty carafe back to the counter where Tamara was already starting to cook more food. I whispered, "Can I talk to you?"

She looked at me, a little shocked before glancing at the table and nodded yes, motioning for me to follow her. She led the way into a huge pantry, closed the door, and turned the utility faucet on. "This won't drown out everything but will make it harder for them to hear us clearly. What's up?"

"You're the only other female that is in the loop. Do you believe what Rook says? That he and Casey and their friends want to help us? I don't want to get anyone's hopes up, especially the cubs, only to find out we have been lied to." I tried not to let the worry enter my voice.

Tamara thought about it for a moment. "I don't know Rook well, but I do know Jonas and his men. They wouldn't help or take orders from Rook if they didn't trust and believe him. Rook used to be a part of this Pride. I don't remember him, but he and Jonas were close. If Jonas believes him, then so do I. We all need hope right now, Jasmine. I choose to believe in that hope. Rook has treated me with nothing but kindness so far, and he gave me a job, something to focus on, which allows me to help the Pride with something I know and love. Food." She paused. "I am not good talking to crowds of people. I get nervous and stammer and shake, but in a kitchen, I can talk through my food. Knowing what I create helps to nourish the Pride, gives me a sense of accomplishment because I contribute to the Pride as a whole. Trust Rook, I do."

I smiled at her. "Thank you." I wanted to hug her but refrained. She turned the water off, took a can from the shelf without looking, and exited the pantry. I followed, grabbing something random from the shelving as well.

"Jasmine, I'll have cinnamon rolls ready to take to the cubs soon if you want to help me," Tamara informed me as she began working at the stove again.

"Great, I'll grab another cup of coffee." I took the fresh pot to the table, refilled my mug, and doctored it the way I like, studying Rook from the corner of my eye as he continued to eat. In the deep recesses of my mind, my cat perked up and purred for the first time in many years. I mentally chided her, reminding her that this man would need a strong woman by his side, not some broken, used up, crazy shifter. She growled back, and I mentally slammed her door, locking her back in her cage.

Chapter 5

Rook

Thinking about talking to Mack and Casey turned the food I ate to cement in my stomach. I couldn't put it off, though, because I needed more help than I had sitting at this table with me even though their willingness to do whatever was needed to get this Pride fixed made me smile. I glanced at Tamara working hard at the stoves and realized how much she had come out of her shell in the last twelve hours. She simply needed a task she enjoyed, which also helped the Pride as a whole Jonas had been paying particular attention to Tamara. Jumping in to help fix the kitchen so that she could cook for those in need. He had begun escorting her to and from her house every day. Most recently, he had started growling at any male who approached her. I trusted Jonas' instincts, and it looked like his inner cat had found their mate. That relationship is one I would be encouraging. Individually, they were assets to the Pride, but together, I could see they would be an unstoppable force this Pride would need.

"I am going to update Mack and Casey. Then, I want to address those at the gates and determine if they are part of the Pride, or if they wish to apply to enter the Pride. After that, we need to get to the meeting house and start putting together the teams for repairs, clean up, and whatever else we need. The sooner we get this Pride working together, the faster we can eliminate all reminders of Tomas and his evil rule." I made eye contact with everyone at the table, noticing Jasmine no longer sat across from me. I searched the kitchen, finding her at the counter, her back to me as she helped Tamara. I opened my mouth to speak to her, but her eyes met mine, and I saw the pain and anguish. She hid it quickly and looked at the floor. That was a habit I would have to break her of. "Jasmine, what would you like to help with?" I realized ordering her may not be the best approach; I waited for her response.

It took a moment and was quiet when it came. "I'll stay here and help Nanny with the cubs. Tamara has cinnamon rolls baking for them, so I'll get them up and fed. Will it be okay if I take them out back into the gardens to play? I think some fresh air and sunshine will do them good." She hunched her shoulders.

She was scared of me and probably of everyone

else. I needed to be gentle with her. I wanted to know what had happened. And I wanted to show her she didn't have to act that way anymore. "That sounds like a wonderful plan." I looked at the men at the table. "Would one of you like to volunteer to guard them while outside? I want the cubs guarded at all times until Mack, Casey, and their team arrives."

Niko spoke up, "I'll stay with them."

Jonas nodded. "Good, and remember, if anything seems out of the ordinary, contact me through the Pride. I'll keep the connection open between only the elite. With this, you won't have to worry about anyone listening in."

"Okay. Finish your breakfast, and then meet me on the front steps. I'll join you as soon as I am done updating Casey," I explained.

***

Chaotic noise drew me to the room where Jasmine had corralled the cubs and felt the excitement emanating from the door. Those cubs were a big reason to stay motivated, to swallow my doubt, and do all I could for this Pride. I turned and walked into the den across from the cubs' room, closed the door, and sank into the closest chair. Breathing deeply, I dialed Mack's number. Quickly calculating the time difference, I cringed; it was only 4:00 A.M. in Missouri.

"This better be good," Mack growled.

"It is, Mack. I need to speak to you and Casey

together."

"Oh, hey, Rook. Hang on, let me wake her. If you can hold for a minute, I have to get Da too, he wanted to be on your next update." I heard Mack stifle a yawn before the phone went silent. Thirty minutes later, I joined Paulo, Jonas, Miguel, and DJ on the front steps. Breathing deeply, the air was full of floral scents and heavy with humidity already, and it was only nine in the morning.

"So, what did the Alpha and her team have to say?" Jonas asked.

"Well, as I predicted, she is on her way here. Jerome has chartered a plane, so they don't have to worry about delays or security checks. Mack and Jerome will be accompanying her. A few others from the Pack are coming to help as well. Jerome is reaching out to a few contacts he has in Rio to help get the therapists we need, and the leader of the coven who works with the Black Mountain Pack is coming to help determine whether the remaining witches want to help or harm. Everyone should arrive tomorrow morning." Knowing reinforcements were on their way, I felt a bit of weight lift from my shoulders. "Today, we deal with those at the gate and get everyone divided into teams at the meeting hall. We need to get a census of who is still here and how many we should expect to arrive over time."

The guys followed me down to the gate. I

surveyed the shifters on the other side. There had to be about three dozen of varying ages and sexes. "Have you come together as a group?" I couldn't tell if there was a leader or not.

"No, but we all came for the same reason," a tall, burly man in front stated.

"And what reason is that?" Jonas asked next to me.

"To find out if the rumor of Tomas' death is true, and if so, to find out if the Alpha is accepting Pride members back."

I looked at Jonas, a bit puzzled. He explained, "Tomas sent Pride members to 'monitor' outposts, as he called them. It was his way of keeping the population here low enough to control. If a shifter showed signs of rebellion, or of possibly growing up to be able to overpower Tomas, he did one of two things. He either sent you to an outpost for a duration of time he determined himself with the potential of allowing you to return, or he sent you to an outpost and eliminated you as a threat, telling your family that some terrible accident befell you." Jonas peered through the gates. "These must be the Pride members who were sent away years ago. At least, the ones with enough nerve to attempt to return, hoping the rumors were true." Jonas' gaze swiveled to the man who had spoken. "Am I right?"

"You got it. So, is it true? Is Tomas dead?" he

replied.

"Yes, he is," I declared. "I don't have time to go over it all again right now, I need to get to the meeting hall. Miguel can get you up to speed, and if you want to rejoin the Pride here, then come to the meeting hall and pitch in to help get the village repaired, cleaned, and ready for the arrival of your new Alpha tomorrow morning." I opened the gate wide enough for myself and Jonas to walk through, the others following as Miguel closed the gates behind us. He gathered the shifters who were waiting for more of the story. At this point, I didn't care what they thought of a female Alpha, they both accepted it and moved forward, or they didn't and left. I would send out the tracking party early tomorrow morning to eliminate any threat hiding in wait for Casey's arrival. I was tired, and my patience was gone. Going forward, there would be no second chances given to anyone.

Miguel joined us at the meeting hall. He had them separated into workgroups before he joined me. "There were a few who were skeptical about a female Alpha, but their fear of being on their own is stronger than the fear of what a female Alpha will bring to the Pride. I have them all working in areas where their strength lies. With this many shifters working on a variety of projects, we need to bring in more security. Jonas, Paulo, DJ, and I can't be everywhere at once."

"You're right. I want you guys to be on Casey's

guard detail every moment she is here. I don't know how long they plan to stay. Do you have anyone you trust in mind?" I asked.

"Yeah, I was training a group before you arrived who will be perfect for the job. There are about twenty of them, which should be enough to cover all the projects. I also want you to think about setting up a camp just outside the perimeter for anyone else who shows up claiming to be from a Pride outpost, or who simply wants the chance to join or wants to see the first female Alpha. Once word gets out, we are going to be flooded with nosy shifters trying to catch a glimpse," Miguel rattled off.

"Okay, I'll place you in charge of the guard and encampment. Take what supplies you need and let me know if there is anything we don't have that you require. You can find me here. This will be the base of operations for the village until we have it up to my satisfaction."

"You got it, boss." Miguel took off.

"Hey, Rook, I've got you set up back by the kitchens." Jonas approached him. "Tamara should be joining us soon. She wanted to get lunch prepared so Jasmine and Nanny could have a picnic with the kids today."

"Great. I want her to get started on the kitchens immediately. I have the electricians checking the wires, and repairing or replacing what they need to bring it up to code. Have her take an inventory of the pantry and get it to me. I'll call in an order to be delivered when Mack and Casey get in tomorrow." A pitcher of water and glass were placed at my elbow, and I quickly downed a glass and refilled it. "This reminds me, make sure plenty of water is delivered to each crew. I don't want anyone becoming dehydrated. We also need a couple more females to help with the cubs. Put some feelers out and have anyone interested come see me today." I furrowed my brow in concentration as my list seemed to grow by the second.

Jonas cleared his throat. "Rook, I have one of the witches our Pride works with here as well."

My head shot up. I hadn't wanted to work with any of them until ours had a chance to vet them.

Jonas held his hands up. "Hold on, she is trustworthy. Probably the only one right now. She wasn't part of the black magic ring Tomas created. She wants to help you communicate with us through the Pride magic."

I stared at her. "And how are you going to do that?"

She squared her shoulders and peered straight into my eyes. "I can't do it permanently, but I do have a spell that will allow you to access the Pride magic for a short period of time, probably long enough to get you through until the new Alpha and her witch get here. A more permanent solution can be created when you pledge your fealty to her within the Pride."

"Will you do it here in front of anyone who walks through?" I challenged her.

"Anywhere you like. I have the herbs I need in my bag, and Jonas has agreed to supply the drop of blood I'll need."

"No blood magic, nope." I jumped to my feet.

"Hold on, Rook," Jonas soothed. "This isn't blood magic, and she needs my drop of blood simply for the Pride magic stored within. I've done this before, Rook. It's safe."

I stared at Jonas for a few minutes. My head pounded in rhythm with the shifter hammering in the kitchen behind me.

"I have a tonic that will help with that headache as well," the witch added.

"What's her name?" I asked Jonas. I knew I could ask her, but I wanted to see if this slight would upset her. If there was any flash of anger across her face, she would be removed and never allowed to come back. Witches can be helpful when they are loyal, but they were extremely dangerous when they worked against you.

"Her name is Lilly," Jonas answered.

I watched Lilly as he replied. She stayed as serene as the moment she approached me. No anger, the only reaction I saw was compassion. "Do I pass the test?" she joked. "I really don't mean you any harm. I know that the female Alpha is on her way, and I know there are forces outside this compound that want her eliminated. I am here to help prevent it any way I can." She laid out the items she would use in front of me on the table. "Will you allow me to help you?"

I glanced at Jonas once more for confirmation, at his nod, I agreed, "Yes, if it will make communication faster and easier with my guards."

She nodded in agreement. I watched her combining the herbs in her mortar and grinding them with her pestle. She recited a prayer over the bowl as she worked, adding in sprinkles of water and then reached out for Jonas' hand. With a small dagger procured from a sheath at her hip, she pricked his fingertip and squeezed a few droplets into her bowl. Stirring the concoction, she again repeated the words. She dipped a tiger eye pendant into the bowl, using it to stir as she closed her eyes and recited an incantation. When she finished, she pulled the pendant out and looked at me.

"As I said, the magic in this pendant will only work for a couple of days to keep you connected to the Pride magic but continue to wear the stone as it will help you to see things clearly without illusion and will help keep you grounded and free from the pull that great power brings with it. Wear it beneath your shirt against your heart where the human and tiger soul rest together." She held the pendant out for me to take.

Rook

I placed the chain over my head and let the pendant slip below my shirt. When the stone hit my skin, I felt the magic disperse through me. Lilly smiled at me. I looked at her, tilting my head, and asked, "How did you know my animal was a tiger? I haven't shifted since arriving."

"That's another gift of mine. I can read shifter souls. I know what animal you were before we were introduced."

"That's a valuable talent to have." I sat back down. That talent opened up a few possibilities for me as well as for Casey when she arrived. "Please don't go far, I may have a proposition to speak to you about soon."

She bowed slightly and moved off to an unoccupied corner, pulled out a book, and relaxed, seeming to be completely available whenever she would be needed. I thought about how her ability to read shifter souls could help when meeting with Pride members who wished to stay as well as potential members when they arrived. Being the first Pride or Pack with a female Alpha would draw all kinds of weirdos, but I believed when everything smoothed out, Casey would prove that gender didn't matter when running the Pride.

I felt a tug on the Pride magic inside, and I turned to see Jasmine walking into the building. I admired the jeans she wore today. They hugged every curve, encasing her long, lean legs. My eyes slowly followed the lines of those legs upwards, catching just a glimpse of skin between the top of her jeans and the bottom of the t-shirt she chose to wear. The emerald green a compliment to her blonde, almost white, hair and deeply expressive eyes. She searched the crowd until her eyes landed on me. A smile lit up her face as she made her way to the table I had commandeered as my desk for the day. I gestured for her to sit before she even spoke.

My heart felt a bit lighter while looking at her, knowing she had escaped the harem life. The stories I heard last night would haunt me for a long time. Her eyes danced with laughter, but I didn't care. Her shoulder-length golden-white hair was streaked with darker shades of brown. One thing I learned from the women last night was that they all kept their hair about the same length. Tomas preferred long hair, the more there was, the more he could hold and hurt them. If they kept it shorter than shoulder length, he punished them severely. I assumed that was why Jasmine's kept hers that length. Her eyes were green with specks of gold, round, and framed by dark full lashes. I wondered what she shifted into, her scent was elusive. All I could pinpoint was cat, but the specific species wasn't there. It was a rare occasion I couldn't scent someone's inner species. She was a mystery I wanted to solve. The tiger inside couldn't wait to find out. The more I studied her, the more attentive he became as well.

My nostrils flared as we took in her scent. He wanted to rub against her and ravage her at the same time. At that moment, he wanted to be free more than my human side. Jonas slapped a hand on my shoulder, breaking the trance I had settled into. I glanced up at him, thankful for the brief distraction. Returning my gaze to Jasmine, I spoke first, "What can I do for you?"

"Niko told me to come down and talk to the women who wanted to help with the cubs, though I don't know why he wants me to talk to them. He said Jonas told him they were ready to come help, so I'm here to show them where to go." She kept her eyes averted.

I looked at Jonas. "Where are the women she needs to talk to waiting?"

"They are outside under the canopy." He glanced at Jasmine. "They aren't all women; there are a few men who would like to help as well. I eliminated anyone who I didn't feel would be good with the cubs, and those I felt who weren't the right influence. Anyone remaining has passed my test and now needs to pass yours."

"Mine? Why me? I thought I was simply helping out and bringing up the ones you had chosen." Jasmine appeared confused.

I turned back to her. "I should have asked you first before assuming you would want the role." I took a deep breath. "Those cubs need an advocate. Someone who will always have their best interest at heart and be their line of defense until they are old enough to speak for themselves. They need an education, proper meals, hygiene, and caregivers who will love and nurture them. I thought since you also know what they have been through, how they have been mistreated, you would have a keen sense of how they feel and help them to open up to other adults as well. Would you be interested? It would mean you would be in charge of all those caring for the cubs."

Jasmine stood and paced back and forth in front of me. "Why me? I'm not a leader. I'm probably just as broken as those kids are. Why would anyone listen to me?" Her eyes flicked up to mine and back down again. At that moment, I saw the fear and uncertainty, the lack of confidence in herself.

"You may see yourself as broken, but let me tell you what I see." I stood and grasped her shoulders. She stiffened at the contact, but I didn't let go. "I see a strong, passionate woman who would rather die than see anything happen to those cubs. I see a shifter who would rip apart anyone endangering those cubs. I see a caregiver who loves to cuddle with them and tell them stories, who loves to watch them discover things about the world, seeing the excitement light up their eyes." I squeezed her shoulders, watching as her eyes lifted back to mine. "My cat senses another strong feline inside you, and he agrees with everything I've said. I have faith in you." I dropped my hands and stepped back. "But it's your choice."

Jonas came around the other side of the table to join us. "Jasmine, I knew the moment Tamara and I walked in with food last night that taking care of those cubs was your calling. You didn't hesitate to instruct us where to set things up, and you gently asked if I would help with the boys' baths. You didn't even realize what you had done in your own soft and loving way, and I didn't think to challenge you either. That's the stuff a leader is made of. It's what you are made of."

"I don't know." Jasmine started pacing again.

"She wants to, Rook, she just needs a gentle nudge. Commanding won't work with her; gentle encouragement will help bring her out of her shell. Suggest that she meets the people who want to work with the cubs. If it doesn't kick in, then we may have to consider putting someone else in charge. Unfortunately, we don't have time to baby her into it," Jonas suggested.

I opened my mouth to respond when I realized I had heard him in my mind through the Pride bond. I smiled. *"Looks like the witch's magic worked. I agree, but I think she'll decide before she gets to the group. Just give her another minute."* I turned and sat back down, shuffling papers around until I found what I was searching for. "Another option we have is this." I handed her the pamphlet.

"A boarding school for shifters?! Are you crazy? We can't send them away; they need their Pride to make them feel loved not like they are in the way or can be sent off and ignored," Jasmine huffed. She glared at me, and I could almost see the wheels spinning in her head until she realized what I had done. She dropped her eyes and her shoulders. "You…you…you did that on purpose. Fine, I'll do it. I may screw it up, but I'll do it. Jonas, show me where the group is so I can talk to them." She glared at me. "That was not nice, not nice at all." It was the first time she had really shown any backbone.

I laughed as she walked out with Jonas. She had spunk; I liked spunk. My tiger chuffed in agreement. With all the emotion going on, the long travel, I needed to let him out to run soon, preferably before Mack and Casey got here. I'd have to grab one of the guys and go for a run tonight. I made a mental note to ask DJ, he was the most aloof of the guys Jonas had suggested. I needed to get to know him better before fully trusting Casey's security to him.

Chapter 6

Black Mountain Pack

Casey

"You can't take the whole closet." Mack sighed in exasperation. I had been rushing around, trying to pack since we had gotten off the phone with Rook. "Please, sit down and eat something. Whatever you forget, we can get on the way or while we are there. This is just a quick visit. Right?"

"Yeah, a quick visit, unless they need us longer. I am their Alpha now. I hate to leave all the choices to Rook, and that sat phone sucks on a good day." I continued to shove things into yet the fifth bag I had found.

"Casey, we talked about this. I thought we

decided not to stay down there. That we would visit, see what the Pride needs, get the resources put into place for them, then come back home 'til the cub is born," Mack reminded me.

I stopped in front of him. "I know what we talked about, but, Mack, I have to do what my gut tells me, and it tells me to pack for just in case." I continued searching for something, my voice echoing out of the closet. "Is Jaxson ready to go, and are we bringing Marla, too? Did your dad contact the therapist he knows who retired to Rio? Are the supplies Rook asked for already on their way?" I emerged, arms full of sundresses and sandals.

"Yes, yes, and yes, Casey. Relax." Mack stood and took the clothes from me, dropping them on the floor and scooped me into his arms. "We leave first thing in the morning, and I don't want to waste the night packing. I would rather spend it wrapped in my mate's arms." He devoured my lips as he lay us both on the bed.

"Mmm. That sounds better than packing to me, too," I purred, wrapping my legs around his hips.

Mack took his time with each button on my blouse. Releasing the final one, he peeled it off my shoulders.

I shot to a sitting position, grabbing my temples, knocking him backward on the mattress. "Ohhhh." I sucked in a breath and rubbed my temples. The sensation lasted a few moments and then was gone. "That was weird." I glanced at Mack.

"Are you okay? Is it the baby?" Mack was running his hands over me, trying to find what had pained me.

I pushed his hands away. "No, the baby is fine. It was like a pull at the center of my Pack magic. I've never felt it before except when I killed Tomas and the Alpha rank fell to me. It was sort of like that shift but not as heavy. Almost like sucking something through a straw and then stopping," I tried to explain.

Mack thought a moment. "It wasn't through Pack magic, I would have felt that." He rubbed his chin in thought. "Maybe it was Pride magic. Someone pulled on Pride magic. Can you tell who it was? Close your eyes and concentrate. Da can always tell who pulls on Pack magic, you might be able to do the same with Pride magic."

I closed her eyes and delved into my mind. Pack and Pride magic looked like sparkly spider webs. I had been practicing the ability to single each one out so I could call on one particular Pride mate at a time if I needed. My web was more complicated because I had two that melted into one: my Pack web, which fell into place when I mated with Mack, and the Pride web that enveloped me when I defeated Tomas and was declared the new Alpha.

I danced along the web, searching and found

one string slightly brighter than the rest and followed it. I smiled and retraced the web in my head. I opened my eyes. "It's okay, Mack. It wasn't anything big. But I think I'm going to like this girl when I meet her."

"A girl pulled on your Pride magic?" Mack scoffed.

"Yup, she sure did, and she doesn't even know what she truly is. I honestly can't wait to meet her. Now, let's forget about Pack/Pride magic and get back to enjoying each other." I crawled onto Mack's lap.

"Whatever my mate wants," he replied and returned to the mattress with me.

Chapter 7

South American Pride

Rook

$\mathcal{I}$ found DJ on the perimeter of the village, giving instructions to a few men I recognized from the meeting the night before. I stopped to observe his leadership skills. A lot could be determined about a man's character by watching him when he was unaware. DJ was very militaristic in his movements and stance, authoritative without malice. As I stood there, he stopped and sniffed the air, spinning around to find me scrutinizing him. He motioned for me to join them.

"Hey, Rook. These are the men who will be patrolling the perimeters." He made introductions, and I took note of each scent. There were two panthers, two tigers, a cougar, a lynx, and the last had me taking a double whiff because I didn't expect to find a bear in the jungle. "I have set up a rotating schedule, so the border is never left unguarded."

I nodded in approval. "It looks like you have things well in hand. I came to see if you had a bit of time to talk when you finish."

"Of course, give me a couple of moments to wrap this up, and I'm all yours," DJ replied, turning back to his crew to complete his meeting.

I let my tiger rise to the surface since his senses are more sensitive than my human ones. As he prowled under my skin, I strolled along the outskirts of the meeting, and when he found nothing to alarm him, we both settled to wait for DJ to join us.

After the crew disbanded, DJ walked the few steps over to me. "What can I do for you?"

"How long have you been with the Pride?" I inquired.

"Ten years," DJ answered.

"How have you not been influenced by the evil that consumed Tomas?" I really wanted to know. That long under a malicious leader would change most men. I stayed silent while he replied.

"It wasn't easy, but I give all credit to Jonas. He took the brunt of Tomas' anger and temper. He sheltered most of the guard from it. He also took the demands and twisted them so that Tomas would get the result he wanted except Jonas did it in a firm yet rewarding way." He took a breath. "You should know since you are also prior military that to keep your men working for you, willing to die for you, then you as a leader have to put your soldiers and team first. That is what Jonas does. If we need anything, he made it happen and took the heat for it from Tomas. If any of us should be jaded and evil, it's Jonas."

I nodded as he spoke. I did understand what it took to keep a team devoted to you. Jonas and I had been two of a five-man team who spent years working together on missions. We were the shadows that entered, annihilated, and left before you could blink. We left that life when we lost two of our team during a mission that was a trap. We realized it a moment too late. Hearing the way DJ spoke of Jonas, confirmed that DJ was a trustworthy ally. "So, you know this jungle like the back of your hand?" I stated.

"Yes, sir. Every inch, every potential hazard, hiding place, or possible ambush," he said with confidence, his chest expanding.

"Good. I need to let my tiger out to run and need someone who can show me the closest safe place to do so and who will run with me as a safety precaution. For the next hour, that will be you." I smiled.

I followed DJ through the dense forest for a good five minutes when he stopped and turned to me. "We can shift here. I'll show you where the best running grounds are. We are still within the border of the Pride, and the guards are already at their posts on this side of the village." We both divested ourselves of our clothes, folding them and hiding them in the crevice of a tree. Moments later, shaking out my fur and stretching, I was ready. My tiger was happy to be let free. DJ stared back at me through the eyes of his panther, gauging my readiness. When he was satisfied, he took off, and I followed.

We were soundless on the pads of our paws. DJ was sleeker and more agile than I was, showing off by jumping up and running through the branches of the trees above. My tiger, being bulkier and heavier with muscle, didn't have the ability to climb as high as him, but I didn't care. *"Show off."* I laughed, grateful for the spell the witch had performed, which allowed me to speak through the Pride magic. I followed on the ground as DJ flew through the trees. The scents and sounds of the jungle around us a symphony that played as we ran. The humidity became oppressive and uncomfortable, slowing us down to a walk. I could smell the small prey around us. A rabbit scurried in fear to find his burrow while a deer munched on the low hanging foliage up ahead. My tiger wanted to hunt. "*Hungry?"* I asked DJ.

"Let's do it," he responded. I could sense his excitement at the anticipation of a hunt. We both crept along, stalking our prey. Him from the trees and me on

the ground. He ran through the trees until he was on the far side of the deer, and I crouched mere feet from the animal, hiding among the fern leaves. I was on its downwind side, keeping it unaware of my threat. "*I'll send it your way. Ready?*"

"*Yes.*" My tail swished, the muscles in my legs coiling to pounce. DJ jumped down from his perch, startling the deer. The deer headed my way, unaware of the threat in its path. I waited, letting my tiger choose the moment to strike. I exploded from my hiding spot just as the deer passed, toppling him from the side, my jaws clamping down on its neck. The more it fought, the deeper my teeth went. I could taste the metal of its blood as my fangs found its jugular. DJ sank his claws into its flank, and his jaws found its spine, breaking it with a shake of his head.

The deer proved to be enough for both of us to fill our bellies and leave enough for another. "*Who is the closest guard to our position?*" I asked as I licked my paws clean.

"*The closest guard is twenty feet to your left.*"

"*Great.*" I stood and began dragging what was left of our meal toward his location. It took DJ a moment to realize what I was doing and quickly joined me, helping me move the carcass. We came upon the guard, who had his gun raised at first until he recognized DJ. I let go of the deer and sat waiting. The guard looked at DJ, nodding once.

He kneeled, leaning his head to the side, exposing his throat. "Thank you for providing this meal, I pledge my loyalty and protection to you and to our new Alpha, Casey."

I roared in response. *"It's time we return, DJ. Tell him he may partake when we leave."*

"You can tell him as well. Your Pride bond spreads to all the guards."

"I know, but we must keep the ranks in order. You report to me, he reports to you. He has sworn his fealty, but he still needs to get instructions and orders from you. There may come a time when both Casey and I will be away, I must have confidence the Pride will respect the authority of those I leave in charge." I turned and walked away, heading back toward the village. I knew DJ would catch up and that the other guards around were alert. I let my tiger take control and race back to our clothes. His joy filled me as we ran, tiger and man as one. I was lacing my boots when DJ emerged in just his fatigue bottoms wiping the sweat from his chest with his T-shirt.

"Thanks for the run. I need to check in with Jonas. Will I see you at supper?" Having spent the last hour with DJ, I felt better about his leadership and the men he chose to guard the Pride.

"Yes, I am going to go check the other guards and then help with the repair crew. If we work hard through the day, we should have all the roof repairs that need to be done finished before the Alpha arrives."

"Good. Casey and her mate should be here for supper, along with those traveling with her. The next few days are going to be rough, so the guards need to be on high alert. Make sure to do a run through the camps outside the border as well. I want any security threat dealt with before she arrives."

"Affirmative."

I'd waited for his agreement before heading off to find Jonas.

Jonas was in the kitchen with Tamara. I almost didn't recognize the place. All of the exposed wires were now out of sight, the ceiling was repaired, and everything was in order. Tamara was instructing men on where to place the supplies that had arrived, and Jonas was working a few feet away. In the last twenty-four hours, I had seen Tamara only once without Jonas as a shadow. My instincts told me it wouldn't be long before he claimed her as his mate; however, she seemed to be oblivious to his attentions so far. I smiled to myself. That would be interesting to watch.

Jonas finally noticed me standing in the doorway. "Hey." He came over, wiping his hands on a rag. "How did it go with DJ?" His eyes never leaving Tamara's movements as we spoke.

"Good. You made a wise decision by putting him in charge." We watched Tamara work. "Does she know yet?" I asked.

"No, but she will. She hasn't stopped long enough to listen to her cat. I don't want to scare her away, but I don't know how much longer I can hold off. My panther screams to claim her every time we are near. I have to busy myself with odd jobs to keep my hands from grabbing her and throwing her over my shoulder." He laughed.

"I am sure Casey will help that along when she gets here. The mating need is thick in this kitchen, and this Pride needs solidly mated pairs to move it forward. Tomas prevented that for years. This Pride is broken because of that." I clapped him on the shoulder. "I'd love to see you two be the first to mate under the new rule."

"Thanks, man. I had started to believe I'd never find my mate."

I answered the sat phone on the second ring, having to dig it out of the leg pocket of my fatigues. "Rook here."

Mack was on the other end. "Hey, buddy. Just a heads up, we are on our way from Rio. Casey is eager to get there, so we will see you in a couple of hours at most. Da and Jaxson are with us, and Marla is behind us with the supplies in the box van traveling at about twenty-five miles an hour. She's pissed. She drew the short straw, so be ready."

"Copy that. I think she'll calm down once she gets here. I located another lynx in the Pride, the only male lynx so far. Maybe we can hook them up, and she can relieve some stress." I smiled at Mack's bark of a laugh. "See you soon." I disconnected and turned to Jonas. "We have two hours."

Chapter 8

Rook

$\mathcal{I}$ returned to prepare the house for their arrival. I had entrusted the cub care and removal of all things Tomas from the house to Jasmine. I hoped I hadn't placed too much responsibility on her shoulders too soon. She had assured me she was fine and didn't have near the damage the other women from the harem did, but I had my doubts. What I found waiting for me when I walked through the door floored me. I was not prepared to see the cubs and the women working together and laughing. My heart swelled at the joy I saw, and a grin broke out on my face.

A few of the women and cubs noticed me standing in the hall and gave me a small smile I scanned the room for Jasmine. We found each other at the same instant, and realization crossed her face. She held up one finger, indicating for me to give her a minute. I nodded back, letting her know I understood. I watched her hurry across the room to the group of women, a few of the cubs following her. She crouched down and addressed them. I didn't want to invade their privacy, but as acting Alpha, I had no choice, so I did just that, listening to Jasmine comfort the women and the cubs.

"You are doing a great job! I need to go talk with Rook, and I could use your help. We want to have the house ready for the new Alpha. The new FEMALE Alpha," she stressed. "Come, you and the cubs work on the sunroom." She stood and led them out a door at the back of the room that led into the sunroom running along the rear of the house. I knew it would be one of Casey's favorite rooms, and a good choice to have ready for her. I watched Jasmine close the door and approach me, her eyes downcast again. There were still a few cubs and three women left cleaning the room we were in.

"I'm sorry about that, I'm trying to keep them busy. They are still skittish around men. Even though you sat and listened to them, it's still hard for them to trust. Getting them working, especially with the cubs around, has helped today; however, they are going to need a lot of help and a lot of time away from the males in the Pride." She still wouldn't meet my eyes.

Rook

"I understand, but we can't sequester them from all men. Jerome will want to meet with them, and they will need to speak with me on a regular basis as well. I can keep the rest of the Pride males away until a therapist deems them ready to rejoin the Pride, though." Jasmine nodded. "You have done an amazing job here. I almost didn't recognize the place when I walked in."

Jasmine looked up and smiled with pride. "Thank you. We have worked really hard. You aren't the only one who wants to rid this place of any reminder of Tomas." She moved to a couch, motioning me to join her. There was a cardboard box sitting on the coffee table in front of us. "I did save a few things I found along the way. I didn't know if you would want to keep them, but I didn't want to just throw them away. These are things, pictures and albums and such, that have Cecilia and an infant who I think is Casey." She pulled out a couple of photos from the box. "I think these are with you. You haven't changed a bit." She smiled as she peered at the pictures.

I took the photos from her and studied them. She was right. "I remember when these were taken. It was one of the few times Cecilia was allowed to take Casey out into the jungle for a picnic. I was always required to go, always on guard. This time, Casey wanted to stand guard with me, so I placed my beret on her head and proclaimed her guard for the day." I stared down at the picture. Cecilia had taken it. I stood at attention, my eyes were on Casey, though. She was smiling straight at the camera and her mother. The beret, obviously too big and listing to the side, covered one of her eyes. "I think she'll love this. Thank you for saving it." I placed the pictures back in the box. I angled toward her on the couch. "Give me a rundown on where you are with the house."

She fidgeted before responding, "The guest rooms have been cleaned and prepared for arrival. I don't want to put Casey in the old master suite until we can completely redecorate it. I couldn't ask the women to go back in there quite yet. I think we need to close it up for now." I nodded, encouraging her to continue. "You can see the difference in here. We took down all the draperies, got rid of all the inappropriate paintings, and we dug into everything that had been put in storage in the attic. I let the kids help with that, choosing what they wanted to see and use." She motioned around us.

I had noticed the change. It was much brighter, and there were a variety of blankets and quilts covering the chairs and couch, bringing a warmer feel to the room. In a corner, an old wooden crate had been brought in and filled with toys, games, and anything the cubs would want to play with. The area rugs had been changed out, too. I liked the changes and told her so "It looks great and feels much more inviting. Where else have you worked?"

"The only other room we really worked on is

the sunroom. Tomas didn't use it much, so it doesn't have his overpowering male ego stamped on it. We brought in the wicker furniture from outside, cleaned all the cushions, and moved a few of the low tables and lamps out there. The windows have been cleaned and sparkle now." Jasmine took a breath, and I could see the sweat on her forehead and the slight tremor in her hand. "The den is going to be the hardest. None of the women or cubs want to go in there."

"That's okay. I am sure Mack and Jerome can handle clearing it out. We will let Casey decide what she wants to do with that room." I could see a question in her eyes. "You can ask me anything, what are you holding back?"

"It's about the third floor." She lowered her gaze.

"Go ahead," I gently encouraged her.

"I want to move all the cubs to that room, along with the women I brought back to help care for them. I want to take the coverings off the windows, paint the floors, and bring in bunk beds for them all. Give them their own space with light and happiness." She held her breath.

"I don't see a problem with that," I replied.

She looked up. "I didn't know if the new Alpha would want to have them in the same home as her. Tomas kept them in the basement because he didn't want to see them, but he didn't want them too far from him." She shivered.

"Make a list of things you'll need to make it happen. Furniture, bedding, rugs, whatever it is. I'll get it ordered and delivered as soon as possible." I agreed with her, those cubs needed happiness and love in their lives, and keeping them together and safe was a priority.

Jonas cleared his throat from the doorway.

"Give me another moment, Jonas, I'll meet you in the den when I am finished here," I acknowledged him, my eyes never leaving Jasmine.

"You got it, boss." Jonas left.

"There's more you haven't said, Jasmine. Spill it." I took her hand in mine. We both gasped at the electricity sizzling between us. Her eyes shot to mine.

"The other women. They need help, lots of it. More than I can give. I don't want to send them back to their room, but we don't have anywhere else for them right now, and there aren't enough guest rooms ready to give them one of those." Her eyes pleaded with me, but she was still hiding something. I searched her eyes, trying to get past her walls. Then it hit me. The women weren't the only ones who needed help. Even though she came to me when I asked for help, she had still been a part of the harem, no matter how short her time in it was, it still had to have affected her too.

"Go choose a room now. One big enough for all of you. Isn't there one near the stairs to the third floor?"

She nodded. "Good, take that one. Send a list of what you need to get it ready, and I'll find it among the shifters here, and we will have it ready by nightfall. If the women don't want to meet Casey right away, let them help with the cubs' room until Casey gets settled. BUT, let them know she will want to talk to them soon." Jasmine leaned toward me in her excitement. I grinned, not wanting to scare her. It took all I had at that moment to hold myself and my tiger back. We both wanted to hold and comfort her.

"Thank you!" She smiled shyly.

I stood and went to join Jonas in the den. I really didn't like this room, but it was the only one available, and one I knew would be private. I shut the sliding door behind me and looked around. The picture windows were covered with thick brown draperies blocking any sunlight from entering. Covering the floor were brown and black shag area rugs. The furniture was sparse with a boxy couch that looked like it was as hard as concrete and two wingback chairs that had seen better days across from it. The only comfortable-looking piece of furniture was a large overstuffed leather club chair. I knew without asking that was the seat Tomas took every time he was in this room.

The furniture flanked a fireplace that I could tell hadn't seen a fire in years. The room was cold in feeling and temperature. Along the back wall was a large ornate desk with built-in bookshelves on both sides of it and a glass display case behind it. I walked over to see what was encased there. This was the first time I had stopped to look at this room.

A wall was full of framed pictures of Tomas with different local dignitaries I assumed as I didn't recognize them. More captured him shaking hands high ranking officials such as former U.S. Presidents, and even one of him and Fidel Castro. Pictures of him and famous actors and actresses such as Angelina Jolie and Brad Pitt. Along with an elegantly framed letter or two, I didn't read them to find out who they were from. A wall dedicated to a sadistic pompous ass. "We need to get rid of all this. Everything in this room needs to be removed and burned." I turned to Jonas. "That's my opinion. I'll leave the final decision to Casey." I looked around for a comfortable place to sit, settling on the window seat in the front of the picture windows. I jerked the drapes open and sat. "What have you got for me now?" I waited for Jonas to fill me in.

"The Pride accountant has been calling. He wants to speak to the new Alpha. I tried to direct him to you, but he won't speak to anyone except Casey."

"That's no problem. She'll be here soon, and Pride finances are one of many things on her list that she wants to go over," I replied.

"He also wants her to go to Rio to meet with him," Jonas added.

"That's a no. He will have to come here. We

can't ensure Casey's safety in a city the size of Rio."
My voice left no room for argument.

"Agreed. I told him as much, but we may have
to send someone to encourage him to join us when he's
invited." He leaned back against the windowsill. "The
kitchen is done and ready for any size gathering.
Tamara has really taken to being in charge there." Jonas
smiled wistfully.

"Have you and Tamara finally given in to the
mating call? Set a date for the ritual?" I asked,
observing the connection they had.

"I don't think Tamara's ready yet. Plus, we have
to get the approval of the Alpha before the ritual can be
done."

"Don't worry about Casey. Once she sees you
two together, she'll willingly give her blessing. I think
you need to tell Tamara, though. If you don't, your cat
will, and he won't be gentle with her. He'll simply
overpower, take, and ask for forgiveness after."

"No shit. He's been telling me that since he
wrapped around her feet at the meeting the first night."

I barked out a laugh. "Yeah, go find her when
we are done. Take her aside and tell her, give her a
chance to accept or deny you before Casey arrives."

"Rook, I'm scared to. What do I do if she
refuses me? I don't think I could handle it." Jonas' face
fell at the question.

"Then you give her some time, win her over,

and give her a chance to let her cat change her mind. When you take her aside, go for a run first. Let your cats play, then tell her," I advised. "How is everything else? Any fighting or dissonance I need to know about or take care of before Mack and Casey arrive?"

"No, amazingly, everything seems to be running well. The Pride is happy to be working to repair and clean up the shit hole they have been living in. Even the rogue camps outside the territory are calm. I doubled the guards on them just to be safe. That could all change when they realize not only is the new South American Pride Alpha here, but she is accompanied by the Black Mountain Pack Alpha."

"Smart. Make sure to rotate the guards. We need them to stay alert. If there are any attempts to breach the territory, I want them to attempt capture first but use deadly force if necessary to protect the Pride."

Jonas stood. "I'll let them know."

I joined him, grasping his forearm in a firm grip. "Now, go whisk Tamara away for a run, brother." I heard Mack through the Pack bond send an update on their arrival. "You have an hour before they arrive."

Jonas pulled me in for a quick hug and clasped my shoulder. "It's good to have you back, brother. I'll see you in an hour." He left through the front door, and I watched out the window. He shifted and took off in a sprint, his tail twitching in anticipation. He'd make it to her faster on four legs rather than two. Tamara was in for an eventful hour. I smiled to myself and went in search of Jasmine to see if she had her list ready for me.

Chapter 9

Jasmine

$\mathcal{I}$ went to check on the progress of the sunroom, happy to see the women working together on something positive rather than cringing in a corner, fearful of when they would be called next. My heart twisted when I thought about how I had lied to Rook. I couldn't tell anyone about my time in the Harem or before. The previous Alpha had taken me as a favorite from the day I hit puberty, even before I was placed with these women. I felt it was my duty to protect them as much as possible, and I made it a point to stand out so I would turn his eye and gain his favor. I was able to take the torture and punishment and box it away, becoming numb to everything. They knew it as well, and we developed a bond quickly. I would do anything for these women, and if taking the pain of his attention saved them a few days of fear, I did it. My shirt rubbed against the still healing scars along my back as I moved, reminding me of what I had lived through.

The cubs came running up to me. "Miss Jasmine, look!" They pointed to a couple of vases full of wilted flowers and weeds. "Do you think the new Alpha will like them?" They asked with hope in their eyes, their innocence showing through. I stroked their hair. These innocent children held my heart, and I never wanted them to go through the hell I did.

"Of course she will, who wouldn't?" I replied, hoping what I said was the truth. "We need to finish cleaning and go upstairs. Rook said you can all live together, so we need to clean the third floor and prepare it for your beds." I smiled.

The cubs cheered in excitement and went to gather their brothers and sisters. My heart filled with hope as I watched them. They would need therapy, as well; a few of them were scared of their own shadows from having lived in that horrible basement for so long. If anyone could help bring them around, I felt it would be Rook. I watched him every chance I got, and the love and compassion that radiated off him when he was around the cubs, confirmed that he would do anything to help them live as normal of a life as possible.

I turned to the woman closest to me. "Sarah, the new Alpha will be here soon. Is everything ready?"

Rook

She kept her eyes to the floor as she replied, "Yes, but..." She stopped herself. They were all so used to having to ask to speak or being punished for attempting to address anyone.

I spoke softly, "Go on, you can speak freely now. What is needed?" I wanted to reach out to her but knew any physical touch would make her clam up even more.

"Do we have to greet the new Alpha?" she whispered quickly.

"No, Sarah, none of you have to be down here when she arrives. Rook said she would want to talk to each of you, but that will be later tonight. For now, you can join the cubs upstairs and help prepare the third floor. I have to make a list of items we need for all of you. Beds, linens, draperies, etc." I cocked my head as I looked at her. "Would you like to help with that?" A tear streamed down her face as I watched. "Sarah, it's okay. You don't have to. I won't make you do anything you don't want to right now."

"No, it's not that. I want to help, but..." She took a deep breath. "I can't write. I never learned. He only allowed a select few of us to be schooled. I wasn't one of them." I realized that admitting that small thing was a big step for Sarah.

"Well then, we will have to fix that. Any of you who want to learn will." I knew making that promise, was above my head, and I hoped I was right. If what

Rook said was true, it would happen. But I had learned a long time ago not to trust what any male said. "Let's gather the cubs and head upstairs. You tell me what is needed and wanted, and I'll make the list. How does that sound?"

Sarah slowly raised her eyes, not quite meeting mine. "I think that sounds good." She turned quickly and gathered everyone, ushering them up the stairs.

"Wonderful. I will meet you all upstairs in a few minutes."

Panic was starting to set in. I breathed deeply, trying to calm my racing heart. Showing any signs of leadership or individualism was a punishable offense. Or had been. That fear was deeply ingrained in me. Rook made me feel that stepping out to care for the others, as I have, was a good thing. I yearned to see him again, to be near him. A voice began whispering in my head. "*What do you think you are doing? You think you can help? You are worthless. A simple toy to be played with and thrown away when used up. Just wait, these men will do the same thing once they realize what you are. A whore to be shared, and that's all. You'll never be more. Why even try?*" I gathered that fear, that voice, that irrational thought and boxed it up, placing it in the closet in my mind with hundreds of other boxes like it. As I mentally closed that door, I heard a small whine, a mewl of sadness. My fears weren't the only thing I had to box up a long time ago. A small tear escaped down

Rook

my cheek as I ascended the stairs.

Miranda Lynn

Chapter 10

Rook

$\mathcal{I}$ went to the meeting house to wait for Mack and Casey, satisfied that the Alpha house would be ready when they arrived. I reached out through the Pride bonds to find Jonas and see how close he and Tamara were to being back. *"Jonas, how close are you guys?"*

"We are a couple of minutes out. Tamara and I will be at the meeting hall in five minutes." His voice sounded full and happy through the bonds.

I smiled to myself. Jonas was deserving of a good mate, and Tamara was the perfect fit. It may take a bit of convincing to get her to feel the same way, but if anyone could do it, Jonas could. *"Good, call in the others so we can greet them properly. See you in five."* I disconnected from the bond. It was nice to be able to speak to him through the Pride magic, but it was a bit more difficult to connect and disconnect. Using a spelled charm to talk was like using a payphone to call overseas: most of the time, the connection was clear, but sometimes, it was staticky and calls were dropped.

The village was a flurry of activity with all the repairs that had been made and the projects underway. Everyone was so busy that no one had time to really stop and contemplate what would happen next, especially with the new Alpha in charge. Excitement coursed through me as I thought about how this Pride would change for the better. I wanted to see all the members work together and see that shifters of any species really could live in peace. The transition would be rocky, I didn't delude myself about that, but I knew it was for the better. Weeding out the evil was a necessity. My cat relished the thought of going on the hunt again. We hadn't been on a hunt like that in a long time. The bloodlust began to sizzle beneath the surface in anticipation.

I strolled around, taking in the changes that had been made in the last few days. Sleep had been elusive with everything that needed to be done before Casey got here. Seeing all the changes made it all worth it. All the houses in the village were getting a fresh coat of paint. The roofs had been repaired and were now safe for the shifters that lived inside. The junk had been cleaned up from around the buildings. Anything deemed usable had been collected on the side of the meeting hall in the center of the village. There was an air of hope swirling around instead of the thickness of fear and depression that I encountered when I arrived. This was a start. You could still sense the brokenness that permeated the Pride, but it would take longer than two days to fix that.

I felt a tug on the Pack bonds and opened to it. *"Rook, are security measures in place? I won't let Casey go any further until I know for sure,"* Mack stated.

"Yeah, everything is secure. Come on in." I smiled. I knew exactly where they were as soon as Mack connected. I looked up into the branches of the trees above us to see the sleekness of both panthers as they jumped down next to me. "It's good to see you both." Casey rubbed against my legs as Mack sat and growled. I knew he was just playing since I was no threat to him. He had claimed Casey, and she, him. "Come on into the building, I have spare clothes you can put on after you change. Your elite are on their way." Casey and Mack followed me and quickly dressed after shifting. "Where is everyone else?"

"Da is still in Rio waiting on the second jet to arrive with the therapist and a couple of other shifters he called in to help. Jax is in the truck about an hour behind us with Marla. The rest are scattered in the jungle and won't ever be seen. We will decide how many we need to leave here when we are ready to go back home." Mack scanned the area on constant alert.

"Hey, Rook," Casey greeted me with a long hug. I wrapped her in my arms, not realizing how much I had missed her 'til that moment. She pulled back and searched my eyes. "You have accomplished a lot in the last two days. I knew you would. Thank you for that."

"It's good to see you both as well. Come and sit, let me fill you in. It's worse than I had expected. Many of the Pride have jumped in to help clean things up, but the Pride itself is severely damaged and will take time to heal and fix." I spent the next hour filling them in on everything, leaving the Alpha house and what I had found inside until the last. I took a deep breath, preparing to share the worst when Jonas arrived with Tamara in tow.

They stood off to the side until I motioned them over. "A little late, aren't you, Jonas?" I teased.

"I thought you might want to tell them everything before introducing us." Jonas turned to Casey and kneeled, bowing his head and tilting to reveal his throat in submission. "I accept you, Casey Badeaux, as my Alpha. I pledge to protect you 'til my last breath, to do your bidding without question, and to protect your Pride as my own."

Casey placed her hand on his shoulder. "Thank you, and I, as your Alpha, pledge to protect the Pride against harm. I pledge to rule fairly and justly. I will put the health and wellness of the Pride above all else." She grinned and stood, gesturing for Jonas to do the same. "It's good to finally meet you, Jonas. I know my father damaged this Pride, and I plan to rectify his actions. I am depending on good members like you to help me." She hugged him, and he had a look of surprise on his face. "Thank you for welcoming me into your family. Now, introduce me to your mate." She looked at Tamara standing behind Jonas.

Jonas put his hand on Tamara's arm, guiding her to stand next to him. "This is Tamara; however, she is not my mate…yet." He smirked as Tamara sputtered.

"Ahh. I apologize for my assumption. Hello, Tamara, it's wonderful to meet you." Casey met Jonas' eyes with a knowing glance. "Let me give you a little advice when it comes to mates. Listen to your inner animal. Don't let your head get in the way of your happiness." Tamara started to kneel, but Casey stopped her. "There is no need for that. I won't make anyone submit in that way. I appreciate Jonas' show of loyalty, and if you choose to do the same after you get to know me and what I plan for this Pride, I will accept it, but not until then." Casey gently encouraged Tamara her with unspoken words. "Now, please, both of you sit with us and tell me what needs to be changed, how you would like to see the Pride work moving forward."

Slowly, over the afternoon, each of the elite guards arrived, each of them pledging their loyalty to

Casey when they arrived. I observed the approval from Mack each time it happened. Casey took it in stride, but I could tell it made her uncomfortable, realizing that every shifter in this Pride would look to her for guidance, leadership, and with doubt. She was the daughter of the devil who led this Pride in fear for so long, plus she was a female, seen as unstable and unworthy to lead. She had a long road ahead of her, but I knew she had the strength to persevere.

I heard a rumble coming down the road and went on alert. I glanced at Niko, who took off with Miguel to meet whoever had made it through the checkpoints. I assumed it was Jax, but we couldn't be too careful. I am sure the word was already out that the first female Alpha was in Pride territory.

"It's Jax. They had to change a flat tire, so it took them longer than expected," Mack informed us.

Mack and Casey went to greet Jax. I pulled DJ aside. "Can you go up to the house and check on Jasmine and the cubs for me? She was supposed to put together a list of things she needed for the cubs' room. See if she has that ready and bring it to me. Once we get Jax and the rest of the crew settled, I want you to take a couple of guys with you to find what she needs."

"You got it, boss." DJ headed off toward the house as I found Casey at the truck.

Jax jumped down, and I grasped his hand. "Glad you made it."

Rook

"Me too, that ride is a rough one. These trucks have shit for suspension. My ass started hurting the moment we turned onto the road less traveled." Jax laughed.

"We don't want to make it easy for the humans to find us," I joked. I made introductions all around and turned back to Jax. "The medical building should be ready for you. Grab whoever you need to unload and get set up. Jonas has already assigned anyone with healing ability to wait for you there. If there is anything else you need, just make a list, and we'll get it on the next trip into the city."

"Sounds good," Jax replied and shook Jonas' hand. "Are we meeting tonight?"

"Yeah, we will have dinner here so the Pride can meet everyone, and then I'll take you all up to the Alpha House."

I watched as everyone became a flurry of activity. Mack accompanied me. "You've come a long way in the last two days, Rook. I'm impressed."

"Thanks, Mack. I wanted to get as much done before Casey came. I knew she wouldn't be able to wait long. I need to prepare you for what she will face at the house." I started walking and shared with him about how we found things when we opened the house. The harem, the cubs, and how Jasmine had become a big part of changing it.

"Sounds like she has been a big help. You speak

of her with a wistfulness, have you possibly found your mate after all this time?" Mack inquired.

"Honestly, I don't know. My focus has been on preparing everyone for Casey. Jasmine has a fire and determination to her that my cat and I both admire, but I think she's hiding something. She says she wasn't hurt in the harem, that she had just recently been put there, but her eyes say different. I think she took on more of Tomas' wrath than she lets on. My cat wants to wrap her up and protect her, but I know she won't welcome that right now."

"I can't wait to meet this girl. The first female to twist you up in knots. Man, just give in to it. The more you try to hold back your nature, the harder it's going to be." Mack slapped my back and grinned. "It's about time you found your mate. Trust me, it will only make you stronger."

I watched Mack with Casey. The little touches they each gave while still focusing on the members of the Pride, assuring each other through the connection that surrounded them and cemented what bonded them together as a team. Their mate bond was obvious for everyone around them to see. My cat purred, telling me he was ready for the same, ready to fill that void inside that had been waiting for years. I couldn't ignore it any longer. My job to protect Casey had now passed to Mack leaving me free to fill in the empty space with the mate it was meant for all those years ago. I looked up at the house, searching the windows for any sight of Jasmine.

Chapter 11

Rook

*T*he next few days flashed by in a flurry of activity. Jerome had been delayed in arriving in the village because of travel delays with the therapist. Three trips had been made into neighboring towns or Rio itself to get the supplies or equipment the Pride required to bring it into this century. Mack and Casey had settled into the Alpha house and met with each of the elite guardsmen. Then they met with each of the females from Tomas' harem. Casey had to take breaks between each one because of the emotional strain it caused. She really cared about each woman, and coming to terms with the fact that it was her own father that had treated them in such a way made it difficult.

With Mack here, I was able to step back from

the leadership role. He came to me on the second day they were here. "So, now that you can take a breath, I have a question for you. We still need you, but rather than assigning you to an area, I want to know where you want to be. What project do you want to work on the most?"

This was a new approach. I was used to simply being put where an Alpha thought my skills would be of the best use. I didn't have to think about this. "I'd like to help with the cubs. They need guidance, love, and a good education. Many of them have missed out on so much, finding the right tutors and teachers for each one is necessary. I would like to help Jasmine do that if it's okay with you and Casey," I responded.

"Casey was right." Mack chuckled. "Then, that project is yours. Keep me updated on the progress and of any requests you two might have. Marla has been with Jasmine since they were introduced. You should find them outside with the cubs now."

"Thanks, Mack." I grasped his forearm in quick thanks and headed out.

"Hey, Rook," Mack called out. I turned, raising an eyebrow in question. "Take things slow with Jasmine. Casey spoke with her last night, and she is more damaged than she portrays. It will take a strong, patient man to get through her shell."

"I know." I sighed and went to join Jasmine and Marla with the cubs outside.

Rook

From that day on, I worked side by side with Jasmine and Marla. We had the third floor of the Alpha house completely renovated. We had, with the help of a couple of shifters with carpentry skills, divided the room into four large rooms. The third floor ran the length of the house; therefore, space was not an issue. On one side of the floor, we had one room for the boys' bunks and one for the girls'. Then, in the middle was a very large communal room with areas for teaching, play, and relaxation, while on the opposite end, was a large room that housed the women who had been in Tomas' harem. It was their safe haven, where they slept, and a living area where they could read, journal, listen to music, or to simply talk. Once a day, in the downstairs sunroom, each woman spoke with the therapist Jerome had flown in.

Marla had surprised me the most. I thought I knew her well, but the side that came out amongst the cubs was new and refreshing. Gone was the bitchy bartender who held people at arm's length. I learned that in another lifetime, before the Pack, she had been a grade-school teacher and special tutor to shifter cubs. Those skills came out, and the cubs brought out a lighter, loving, more fun Marla. The cubs responded well to her, too. By the third day, she had them on a routine that they enjoyed and counted on. The cubs anticipated their lessons both in the communal room as well as outside. Marla had created a plan to teach them both rudimentary skills as well as their shifter skills. With the help of a few of the witches from the local coven, she was able to pair the cubs with appropriate mentors for their species. Every afternoon, the cubs got to play and practice in the enclosed yard and woods around the house with their mentors.

I loved watching this time as not only did it help the cubs begin to learn and acclimate to who and what they were, they also learned how the Pride worked, each level of the hierarchy, and how to earn it. Beyond that, the adults chosen to mentor the cubs flourished too. The cubs reminded them that you have to play as well as work. They opened up more, becoming more outgoing and a positive influence within the Pride. Jasmine and Marla had done well choosing. I even had two cubs I mentored. The only tigers in the bunch. I was hesitant at first, but Jasmine had coaxed me until I caved and have been thankful ever since.

It took four days before the first challenge to Casey came. Even with all the progress the Pride was making, we knew it was too much to hope it would continue without any hiccups. The challenge came from a shifter outside the Pride, one who had traveled and was living in the camps along the border and thought a female Alpha would be easy to defeat. An easy challenge that would gain him a large Pride to rule.

That challenge was how I found myself in a locked door meeting instead of working with my cubs

Rook

this afternoon.

Chapter 12

Rook

"*I* think you should wait until Da gets here." Mack paced as he spoke.

"Why? If I wait to respond or acknowledge the challenge, I'll be seen as weak, especially if I wait for Jerome. Part of coming down here was to show I am strong enough to be the Alpha, and part of that is facing any challenge head-on. You know how strong I am, you have been working with me every day. Now is the time to show that strength," Casey declared. "Rook, what do you think?"

"I agree with Casey. If she waits, it will only invite further challenges. We need to address this, nip it in the bud, so she can focus on repairing the Pride. You know that the rules of a challenge allow her to choose two shifters to fight with her," I responded.

"Yes, but he gets to choose two fighters as well," Mack huffed.

"You don't think we can take them out? Between you and me and Jonas, she will be able to focus on fighting the challenger and squashing any rumors that she isn't up to the task of being Alpha. We need to face it now."

"Agreed," Casey chimed in. "If I choose you and Rook, we can defeat anyone." She rose and went to Mack, circling her arms around his neck. "I believe in you, and you believe in me. Send Jonas with my answer, and let's set it up for tonight. Give the Pride a good show and shut down any hesitancy there is in the Pride finally accepting me as their Alpha."

Mack encircled her waist and rested his forehead against hers. "I don't want you fighting in your condition. We can use that as an excuse to put him off, at least until the cub is born." He kissed Casey's forehead.

"No, I'll fight tonight. I won't let anything happen to our cub or me, and I know you two won't either." She turned in his arms. "My decision has been made. I thank you all for your council on this matter." She looked at each of us before addressing Jonas, "Go tell him I accept his challenge and will meet him in the clearing at the center of the village tonight. He may pick two fighters to bring with him, but no one else that

118

is not Pride will be allowed in."

Jonas bowed before leaving, and Casey stared at me. "I am depending on you and Mack to take out his fighters. Do not step into my fight unless I call you. I have to take him down myself, or I am not worthy of being this Pride's Alpha."

Casey spun to kiss Mack on the cheek and left the room.

"I don't like it, Rook. This whole challenge feels wrong. I think we need to involve the coven as well. I want to make sure this challenger isn't planning on cheating in any way. Plus, an added protection spell for the cub would set me at ease about the fight." Mack sat, rubbing his face.

"I'll go meet with them now. We won't let anything happen to her, but she is right, she has to defeat this guy on her own for the Pride to fully accept her. Have faith, Mack, I know she can do this." Mack just nodded at me, lost in his own thoughts and worries.

I left, hoping what I said would be true. Casey had only fought once. I knew she had been working with my team back home, and Mack himself, but I didn't know how ready she was. It really didn't matter at this point, she had made her decision, and it was my job once again to help secure her safety and ensure Mack's head was in the fight.

Miranda Lynn
*****

The next few hours were spent in meetings. First, with the coven leader and her two highest witches, discussing what could be done that wouldn't interfere with the fight. It was decided a protection spell could be cast around Casey's womb that wouldn't affect the fight. Then two spells would be cast over the Pride village. One would deaden the sound so the fight wouldn't bring on any spectators we didn't want, and the second would be an alarm spell to help the guards keep a closer eye on the perimeter and would alert the witches and the elite guard to any trespassers. Anyone who attempted to pass through without permission would be temporarily incapacitated, giving the guards enough time to get to the intruders.

I became antsy, wanting to get back and check on Jasmine and the cubs. The more I was around her, the stronger the pull to stay with her was. I couldn't give in to the temptation right now, though, she needed a gentle hand and someone who could focus on helping her work through her problems. I couldn't give her that focus until Casey was solidly in control of the Pride as Alpha.

"Rook, tell these imbeciles to let me through the checkpoint!" a voice roared through the Pack bonds. Shit, that was Jerome, and he was pissed. I grasped the pendant around my neck, feeling how little magic was left. I hoped it was enough to get through to Miguel.

Rook

"*Miguel,*" I called.

"*Yeah, boss, you sound weak, everything okay?*"

"*Yeah, the magic is wearing off. I need you to contact the checkpoint and tell them to let Jerome and his people through before he tears their heads off. He's tired and pissed.*"

I heard Miguel chuckle through the Pride bond. "*10-4 boss, already on it.*" The pendant gave me a small zap, and I knew that would be the last time I could communicate through the Pride until Casey joined us. I needed to remind her that had to be a top priority before the challenge took place.

A Jeep rumbled into the village a little faster than was safe. It skidded to stop at the meeting hall, and Jerome exited the driver's door. "Jesus, that is one hell of a drive." He glanced around, his eyes landing on me. "Rook, you have some idiots for guards out there. I hope that's just a temporary situation." His frustration radiated off him in waves.

"Yes, for now. They are loyal and accepting of a female Alpha. They also have the skills needed to guard, though maybe not the brains to differentiate such." I bowed my head to the side in submission. Jerome was also radiating Alpha power, which made my cat cringe.

A female in stilettos and a tailored business suit got out of the passenger side and walked around the front of the Jeep, placing her hand on Jerome's arm. "Jerome, you need to calm yourself. If you don't, you'll have everyone in a five-mile radius on their knees." She seemed so out of place in the jungle with her coifed hair, pristine makeup, and manicured nails. Her eyes were hidden behind designer sunglasses, and a slim Gucci attaché had been tucked under her arm.

Jerome took a visible breath, and the urge to submit lifted. "Thanks. Katarina, let me introduce you."

"No need," she replied. "Hello, Rook. Where are the women, and where is Jasmine? I need to speak to her first."

I growled deep in my throat at her rudeness, and my cat agreed with me, growling as well. I looked at Jerome in question. With a sigh, he explained, "Rook, this is Katarina. She seems a bit rude but is the best shifter therapist on the continent. Her time is dedicated to helping shifters get past any trauma they have had and to acclimate to living among humans and other shifters. She is good at what she does, and she knows it. She is also a descendant of a very long line of psychics. Combine that ability with her shifter abilities, and she is the best at what she does, but not so good dealing with people outside her office." Jerome grinned.

"That really was unnecessary, Jerome. He will find out in time. Right now, I need to find Jasmine." She turned to me. "Interesting. Appears your kitty there doesn't like that idea. Are you her mate?" Katarina stepped forward.

I growled, "No, but I will protect her from anyone I feel is a threat."

She stopped right in front of me. "Take a good whiff, and let's get this over with. I am not a threat to you or her. I only want to help. My goal is to see our shifter species thrive and grow, not to wither and die. So take a whiff and then take me to her."

I took a deep breath, filtering through the shampoo, body wash, lotion, and perfume that were layered on her skin. Finding her true scent beneath all of that, I was surprised by what I found. I raised my eyebrows at her in shock. What she said was true, she didn't want to hurt any of the women. She genuinely wished to help them. What shocked me more was the shifter I smelled. "You're a lion," I said.

"Lioness, yes. One of the last alive. I don't advertise it, so please keep that bit to yourself. I only reveal her when absolutely necessary."

"That's why the layers of fragrance." I stroked my chin, still trying to get a good handle on this woman. "Okay, I'll introduce you to Jasmine, but you only stay if she feels comfortable."

"Agreed." Katarina turned and gracefully sat in the Jeep again.

I glanced at Jerome, seeing him still smiling. "Where the hell did you find her?" I asked.

"It's a long story. I'd hop in that Jeep and drive

her wherever you need to. She's not a patient woman and an even more impatient lion. Remember, she could rip you in two if she wanted." He laughed.

I shook my head as I climbed into the vehicle and drove her the short distance to the house.

Chapter 13

Rook

Pulling up to the house, Katarina didn't wait for me to open her door. She got out and walked right in as if she owned the place. I had to hustle to catch up to her. I found her in the foyer, eyes closed and taking deep breaths.

"Bring my bag in from the Jeep. I'll need a room as far from the main part of the house as possible to meet with the women." She breathed again. "I want to speak with the one in charge of the cubs first." She stepped out of her stiletto heels and stared pointedly at me. "Well, what are you waiting for? Chop-chop."

"Look, I don't know who you think you are, but just because Jerome brought you doesn't mean you can order us around as if you were Alpha." I glared at her. I did not like this woman at all.

"I know exactly who I am. I am here to help those in the Pride who are too broken to heal and to help them acclimate to what living in a Pride should be like. I have been requested specifically among the therapists available to your Alpha. I don't have time to wait around, and I don't tolerate bossy attitudes. I may be abrupt, and for that, I apologize." She smiled. "I would greatly appreciate your help in my requests," she added with sarcasm.

Realizing it wasn't worth the time or my breath to argue with this woman, I ran to grab her bag and showed her the farthest guest room on the second floor. "This is as far as I'm willing to place you. The room is away from the main living areas, but close enough to alert me if anyone needs me."

She walked around, inspecting the room. "This will do, I will need two comfortable chairs if you can spare them and a portable room divider if you have one. I don't want the women to see the bed when we chat."

That was probably the first smart thing I heard come out of her mouth. "I'll see what I can have brought in."

"Wonderful, and again, I want to speak to the girl in charge of the cubs. Please send her to see me as soon as you can. The sooner I can start, the better." She turned away from me in dismissal.

I really didn't like this woman, and neither did my cat. Every time she brought up Jasmine, he growled and wanted to pounce. I held back only because she came on Jerome's recommendation, and I knew he wouldn't bring anyone to the Pride that would hurt them. I left her to prepare in whatever way she needed to and went in search of Jasmine.

Jasmine was outside playing with the cubs. I took a moment to observe her. She laughed and chased them in a game of tag, her head thrown back with pure joy radiating off her. My cat purred in contentment watching her. I didn't want to interrupt this time but knew I needed to. I wanted to see her like this all the time, and that wouldn't happen until she faced the demons she lived with every day. The Pride was on its way to healing, but many of the shifters had a long way to go before the process would be done. I approached her as she fell to the ground rolling with one of the cubs. My shadow fell over them, and she peered up at me. I saw the shutters fall behind her eyes instantly.

"Hey." I smiled.

She stood and dusted herself off. "Hi."

"The counselor is here. She would like to meet with you to get a schedule set up for those you feel need the most help first." A little white lie. If I admitted that Katarina wanted to start Jasmine's session right away, she might run.

"Of course. Whatever you need." She motioned one of the oldest cubs over and bent to whisper in her ear. "Okay, I'm ready."

127

Miranda Lynn

"I put her in the farthest room from everyone else. Her name is Katarina. I'll warn you, she is very straight forward and seems a bit short when she talks." I placed my hand on her lower back to guide her into the house. She stiffened at my touch but didn't jump away. I kept my hand where it was. I needed her to get used to my touch and associate it with love, concern, and caring. My cat hated that she stiffened; however, I calmed him with the knowledge we would win her over and be here to help her through her healing process.

Katarina was in the kitchen when we entered, and Jasmine stopped just inside the door. "Katarina, this is Jasmine. She has taken over caring for the cubs and the women who were kept secluded from the Pride." I couldn't bring myself to call them a harem out loud or voice what they had been forced to do.

Katarina walked over, hand extended. "It's a pleasure to meet you, Jasmine. You are much younger than I had imagined." She shook Jasmine's hand. "Would you have a few moments to sit down with me and tell me about the women and cubs here, and help me decide who I need to start working with first?" Her voice was warm and welcoming, her posture as well. She had changed from her business suit and heels into a pair of worn jeans and T-shirt, keeping her feet bare. This version of Katarina was much more approachable and set both myself and my cat at ease.

"Yes, I have time," Jasmine shyly answered.

Rook

"Wonderful. Please, come join me in my room. I am still unpacking. We can talk while I finish."

I followed their movements out of the room until they were no longer in my line of sight. I really hoped this therapist could break through the pain that surrounded the Pride. I took a moment to reflect on what I had seen in the last few days since arriving. There were a lot of markers for PTSD that I hadn't recognized at the time. Many of the shifters had triggers that would set them on edge, making them ready to attack, or the complete opposite, sending them into themselves and unable to function around others. The combination of PTSD and a wild animal living inside you was not a good mix. I had experience in dealing with fellow soldiers with PTSD, but it had been quite a few years. It was time I dug up and dusted that knowledge off. I had no doubt Jasmine suffered from it, among many other things. Therapy would help, but my cat and I would have to approach her a little differently. I wanted her in my life for a long time. She didn't know it, but my cat had already decided she was ours. I agreed.

I needed to talk to Mack and Jerome. If I wanted to be able to help her and court her properly, then I would need to pass some of my duties to others so I could devote the time required. I left the main house, reaching through the Pack bond to find Mack. *"Hey, Mack, do you and Casey have a few minutes? I need to talk to you both."*

"Yeah, man, we were just grabbing a bite with some of the Pride at the meeting hall. Come join us," Mack answered.

Chapter 14

Rook

$\mathscr{M}$ack, Casey, and I had moved to a corner table to talk after they finished their meal. It was as private as we could get considering where we were.

"What's up, Rook?" Mack stared curiously at me.

"Well, after Casey's challenge fight, I would like to delegate some of my duties to Pride members who are ready to take them on. I want to focus more time on helping Jasmine through her therapy." My face flamed with heat.

"I think that is a great idea, Rook. I wanted to suggest that myself, but Mack told me to wait," Casey said. "You have done a great job getting things going in the short time you have been here, but I never intended for you to be a permanent fixture in the Pride. I know you feel more at home in the States, and I want you to return there whenever you feel ready."

"Thank you, Casey. I don't want to leave at this moment, but you are right. The States is home now, and I do want to return. Hopefully, I can convince Jasmine to return with me in time. The Pride is strong, and every day, I see them growing as the knowledge that Tomas is truly gone sets in. There are still a few of his men we need to weed out before I am confident enough to leave. I think your fight tonight will help with that. Are you ready?" I turned my full attention to Casey. My head had been full of Jasmine all day, and I needed to focus on Casey and her upcoming battle. Jazz would be there when Casey had fully established her rule.

Jazz...I rolled the nickname over in my head, and it felt good. She was my Jazz. I would show her that soon enough.

"I am as ready as I can be." Casey smiled. We spent the next hour going over who would be there for her as she faced the challenger. This was going to be a huge gathering, and Mack made sure I had plenty of guards ready to keep the crowd under control. I assured him that all bases were covered. I had even had Jonas place snipers in the trees at sporadic intervals, so we had eyes on the forest for at least a mile out. They would rotate shifts throughout the night, even after the fight, and were instructed to shoot any unknown shifter on sight, inflicting injury, not a killing shot. We wanted to be able to speak with anyone who may be a threat and determine if death was warranted. I was sure there would have to be a few deaths, it was inevitable. There always was when a shift in leaders happened, but we wanted to keep the deaths to a minimum. Casey wouldn't rule by fear like her father, but she wouldn't be a pushover either.

I put Jazz out of my mind for the rest of the day as we prepared the challenge field. Casey would be meeting her challenger at dusk per his request. She chose the place; he got to choose the time. We had less than an hour until showtime. Jonas and the elite arrived on the heels of Jerome and Marla.

"Is everything ready?" Jerome asked.

"Yes, sir. We have the perimeter secured, and Casey has chosen Mack and me to stand with her. Jonas will be ready to jump in if needed. The challenger is no match for Casey, though. This should be a quick fight," I assured him.

"Good."

Casey and Mack joined us in the clearing as her challenger emerged on the other side, two shifters with him. The clearing filled up quickly with onlookers. The atmosphere was charged with anticipation. This was the moment Casey would either prove herself as capable of leading the Pride or not. The match was between Casey and her challenger. Those chosen as seconds were simply here to make sure the fight was fair and to remove whoever lost. We were not to enter into the battle.

Her challenger stepped forward. "I, Maverick, of the South American Pride, challenge for Alpha."

Casey stepped forward. "I, Casey, Alpha of the South American Pride, accept your challenge." She turned to the crowd. "Let it be known that this is the only challenge I will accept. When I win this, it will cement my position as your Alpha. If anyone here thinks to challenge me, my seconds will take you out. I do not have time to fight petty squabbles to prove myself. If you still do not accept me after this fight, then leave or face the threat of being hunted by my elite." She faced Maverick again. "I do not want to kill you, but make no mistake, I will if I must."

They both moved back, and Mack stepped forward. "This fight will be in shifted form, no one is allowed to assist them in any way. The fight ends when one submits to the other, or at the first death, whichever comes first."

Both of Maverick's seconds were in their animal form. Mack chose to shift, as well. We had agreed in our meeting I would stay in human form. Casey rubbed against my leg as she went by.

Maverick charged at her, and the fight began. He was bigger in his tiger form, but Casey was more agile and faster. I could tell Mack and Jerome had been working with her. I was amazed at how much she had learned in the few days since I had left.

She got a lot of nips in as she maneuvered. Maverick was bulky and awkward, trying to use his weight against her. He was slow for a tiger. Teeth and claws raked at each of them. Casey dodged most of his attempts until her paw found a small hole that made her falter for a second, giving Maverick the advantage. As his claws raked down her side, she let out a roar. Recovering quickly, she clamped onto his back leg. Bone snapped, and his hind end went out from under him. The crowd roared in support. Casey saw her chance and charged at his side, rolling him and taking his jugular in her mouth. Standing on his chest, teeth clamped, she growled.

I stepped forward. "Maverick, do you concede?" The two shifters he brought with him paced at the edge of the clearing, pawing the ground and snarling. I looked at Jonas. "Ask him."

"He won't respond, Rook. Letting him live isn't an option," Jonas whispered to me.

"Casey, he has cut off communication with the Pride, if you let him live, he will always be a danger, a threat to you and the Pride. I know you don't want to, but you must kill him." I spoke through the Pack bonds.

Casey whined softly. She clamped down and shook her head, breaking Maverick's neck instantly. Stepping off his limp body, she roared, and the crowd roared with her before they kneeled down with bowed heads. As she was scanning the crowd, the two shifters who came with Maverick, charged to attack. Mack and I weren't close enough to help. What we saw next seemed to happen in slow motion. Three shifters exploded from the crowd leaping to Casey's defense. Two tigers went for the attackers, and a bear knocked Casey down, covering her completely beneath him. All four paws framed her as he roared, challenging anyone to confront him. He moved only after Maverick's friends had been eliminated. He and the other two lay down and exposed their throats to Casey in acceptance. She sat up and lowered her head, accepting their submission.

Mack shifted and ran to Casey's side, checking her for any other injury besides the gashes on her side. I addressed the crowd, "Who will dispose of the challengers' bodies?"

Paul and DJ stepped forward. "We will."

"Good. Everyone else, go home. We will celebrate this win tomorrow. If you still feel that Casey isn't your Alpha, I suggest you leave now." I walked over to Mack and Casey as the crowd slowly dispersed. The shifters who defended her were still there. "Shift so that we can thank you properly."

The bear was the first to shimmer back to his human form. "There is no thanks needed. I will protect the Alpha till my last breath." He kneeled again.

Rook

"Please stand," I heard Casey say behind me. She stood there in a long silk robe with Mack at her side. "I would like to know the name of my protector." She smiled.

"My name is Ben."

"You are not of this Pride, are you, Ben?" Casey asked.

"No, I have no Pride or Pack. I have been wandering on my own for years, searching for the right place to settle. I heard of you and came to see if a woman could truly be Alpha. When I saw you enter into the challenge without hesitation to defend yourself and your Pride, I was impressed. But it was the moment after, when I realized not only did you do what was necessary, you did so even carrying your cub. You put your Pride before yourself, that is what I want in an Alpha. I would like to apply for acceptance into the South American Pride."

"Anyone who puts themselves in harm's way for me will always be welcome in this Pride." Casey smiled. "Join us for dinner tonight, all three of you, and let us get to know you. If you wish to join, you are welcome. We can use good and trustworthy shifters. I believe you are all such." Casey took Mack's hand, and they headed back toward the Pride grounds. Jerome, Marla, and Ben followed, scanning for threats along the way while Jonas and I stayed back.

"What is your choice?" I addressed the two

shifters left. It was then I realized one was female. She stepped forward first.

"We would like to join as well. My name is Nikki, and this is my mate, Stephen." She averted her gaze when she finished.

"Very well, join us. The Alpha would like to get to know you. Come eat and get a good night's rest. Jonas and I will speak more in-depth with you about your position in the Pride tomorrow."

They nodded and headed after the others. "Do you think the threats are done?" I asked Jonas.

"For now. Once word gets around about the fight, and the fact that Casey fought even while carrying cubs, it will show her strength. Threats will always be there, but tonight Casey proved herself and will now have the support of the whole Pride." Jonas smiled and grasped my shoulder. "Now, let's go celebrate with the others."

Chapter 15

Jasmine

A week had passed since the big challenge fight that I couldn't bring myself to attend. I stayed back with the cubs, using them as my excuse. I had been seeing the therapist daily, our sessions were short, but I felt comfortable with Kat. She didn't pry and accepts me as I am without expectations. She was like Rook and actually asked me what I wanted out of life now. I told her I wanted a normal life but didn't think I could ever have one. Kat helped me realize it was possible, but I had to face my pain first. I had to forgive myself and others before I could move forward. *Hah, I probably will never live a normal life then.*

I walked toward her room for today's session and knocked on her door.

"Come on in, Jasmine," she called.

I opened the door to find her room different. The curtains were drawn halfway, making the room dimmer and softer. A chaise lounge had been brought in and placed near the fireplace with the chairs we usually sat in.

"Come on in. I wanted to see if you would be willing to try something different this session." She smiled.

I closed the door behind me and went to my regular seat. "What do you want to try?" I asked a little nervously.

"During our conversations, I have found that you don't want to talk about the past. I understand it hurts too much, and you are afraid to open yourself to that pain again. Today, I want to see if you would be willing to try guided hypnosis."

"What is that?"

"It's a way for you to access your memories in a safe environment. I will be with you the whole time, and you will be in control. I will put you into a calm, hypnotic state and guide you to your through your memories. I have found this to be beneficial for many clients who have experienced trauma like you."

"I don't know." I took a deep breath. "I'm scared to face any of it again."

"I know you are, Jasmine, but until you do, you won't be able to have the life you want or the relationship you hope for. I've seen how you look at Rook and how he looks at you. If you want him, you are going to have to take some risks in therapy to get there, but it's up to you. We will only go as fast as you want." She relaxed, waiting for my response.

I stared into the fire. I wanted Rook, my cat wanted him, too. It was getting harder to keep her caged the more we were around him. He calmed me in a way no other had. I knew deep down that he wouldn't wait for me. He had been so patient this week, but his job was coming to an end here in the Pride. He might be here a couple more weeks, but I understood he would be going back to his Pack soon, and then he would be gone for good. It was time for me to take a chance. If I didn't, I might never get out of the darkness I was in. I looked at Kat. "Okay, let's try it."

Her grin widened. "Great. Do you want to lie down or recline in your chair? Whichever is most comfortable for you."

I chose to lay on the chaise in the sliver of sunlight filtering through the curtains. I pulled a lap throw over my legs and got comfortable.

"Okay, now just take a few deep breaths and focus on my voice. Know that you are safe, you are warm, and nothing in your memories can hurt you ever again. I am here with you, and you can bring yourself out at any time. You are in complete control." Her voice continued in a warm and calm tone until I relaxed.

141

Miranda Lynn

"What is the first thing you can remember?"

I am dirty and hungry in the basement, waiting to see when we would get our next meal. I was maybe twelve. I was well-developed for a twelve-year-old, having more of a figure than my oldest sister down here. I had lived in the basement for the last six years and knew the routine. I didn't know where the older shifters went when they were taken away, but they never returned. The oldest sibling here was fourteen, although she looked about eight. I tried to keep the younger ones busy, telling them made up stories and playing 'hide and seek'. We had to be quiet. If we weren't, we were punished. He would lock us in a small box sometimes for a few hours, but most times, for a few days. It smelled of death and decay, and it usually only took one time to remind us of his rules.

This day the door opened. My stomach growled at the possibility of food, but that's not what was brought. Tomas entered with a shifter I had never seen before. "My daughters, come to me." We all scurried to his request and lined up. "Maverick, you may have your choice." The shifter with Tomas came and inspected each of us, circling us and sniffing at our necks. His breath reeked, and when he sniffed my neck, I could barely contain the shiver that threatened to overtake my little body. He licked his lips at my ear and whispered, "We will have fun, little one." He stood and faced Tomas. "I'll take this one."

142

Rook

"Jasmine, you are safe. It's time to wake up." Katarina brought me out of my memories. My hands shook as I ran them through my hair, pushing it away from my face. "Can you tell me what you experienced? What memory came forward?"

I met her eyes, and in a voice that sounded dead to me, I replied, "It was the first time Tomas gave me to someone as a present. The start of the hell I lived in for so long." Breathing deeply, I went on, "I had forgotten about that first meeting, locked it away, mad at myself because I didn't resist."

"First, you need to acknowledge that you couldn't have. You were nothing more than a child, doing as she was told. Could you have overtaken Tomas or the man you were given to?"

"No."

"First and foremost, you need to forgive yourself. It's okay to admit you were scared, and that what you did, you did out of self-preservation, to make sure you came back to protect those younger than you," Katarina assured me.

"I don't know if I can," I honestly replied. It was true, I didn't know if I could. I was sure the Pride wouldn't.

"That's what I want you to work on before our next session." She handed me a journal. "I want you to take a few minutes every day and write that you forgive yourself, write something good that happened that day,

143

and something that made you feel happy and positive. I know you can heal, and I am here to help, but you have to be willing to work on it as well." She stood and escorted me to the door. "Go play with the cubs, or better yet, go find Rook and take a stroll." She smiled.

I carried my journal with me, deciding to get started now. It was time to take back control of myself and my life. I wandered around, searching for a spot that called to me. I needed to be away from the other shifters, so I headed further into the jungle. I knew that the perimeter was guarded, and I would be safe. I settled into a small grove of ferns at the base of a large tree. I gazed into the limbs thinking it would be a great hiding spot for a big cat.

A tear escaped and landed on the first page of the journal after I had opened it. "Hell of a way to start, Jazz, crying on the first page," I chastised myself. I spent the next half hour writing. Once I got the first few words on the page, they seemed to pour out of me. I realized I wasn't alone when I stopped. I could feel someone watching me. I searched the foliage around me, unable to locate where the feeling was until I looked up into the tree branches above me. That was where I found him in all his tiger glory. He twitched his tail, grazing the top of my head before he leapt to the jungle floor beside me. I sat still while he watched me. It felt like his eyes could see past all my walls and into the darkness, where I hid all the reasons why I felt so broken. There was a mixture of compassion and underlying hunger in his gaze. "Hey, Rook," I whispered, and reached out for him, my hand shaking. He lowered his head, nudging my arm. I ran my hand through his fur, it was warm from the sun and soft under my touch.

Rook lay next to me, turning his head to lick the palm of my hand before lowering it to his paws and closing his eyes. His presence comforted me, allowing me to finally relax. The emotions from that day had drained me, and I fell asleep with the knowledge he wouldn't let anything happen to me.

Chapter 16

Rook

My cat and I watched Jasmine as she slept. She must have been dreaming because her expression twisted as her eyes darted beneath her eyelids. I moved closer, trying to comfort her with my body heat. I had no idea what horrors she was reliving in her dreams or how to make them go away, I just knew I wanted to protect her and banish her fears. I had a long road ahead of me with her, and patience would be the key. I told my cat the same, and although he didn't understand, my human side did. We couldn't claim her yet. She had to accept our claim, and she wouldn't be able to do that until she dealt with her past.

The sun was setting, and I knew we needed to get back to the Pride. I nuzzled her neck, breathing her

scent deep into my lungs and let out a low growl.
Sitting back, I watched her wake up. My heart clenched
as she opened her eyes and met mine. I wanted to watch
her wake up every day. I chuffed at her.

She smiled and stretched. "Hey." Then she
noticed the sun. "Wow, I didn't mean to sleep that long.
I actually didn't mean to go to sleep at all." She hopped
up and grabbed the journal she had with her. "I need to
get back to the cubs." She talked more to herself than to
me. I rubbed against her leg and looked up at her.
"Thanks for staying with me." She couldn't meet my
eyes, her shyness had returned, and she clenched the
journal with both hands. "I'm going to head back." She
turned and started walking. Her steps faltered when I
joined her, but she didn't say any more.

I wasn't going to let her return alone. There
were still dangers out there, and neither my cat nor I
were going to let her out of our sight until we were back
in the village. My senses were on high alert as I
escorted her, always scanning for threats even as I
rubbed against her and playfully flicked her with my
tail. Only when we reached the main building in the
middle of the village, did I relax. Tamara greeted us as
we walked in.

"There you are, Jasmine, I was just heading out
to find you." She glanced down at me. "And hello to
you, too, Rook." She smiled, returning her focus to
Jazz. "Do you have a minute to sit with me? I want to

go over the meal and snack plan I have created for the cubs."

"Sure," Jazz replied.

I nuzzled her hand.

"Thanks for the escort, Rook, I'm safe now."

I wasn't leaving her that quickly. I followed them to the table and curled up at her feet as she sat. I heard her let out a heavy sigh.

"Let him be, Jasmine. If he's anything like Jonas, he's going to stay no matter what you do or say." Tamara laughed when I huffed in agreement. "See, he even agrees with me."

I lay there while they went over the meals and where the cubs would eat. I enjoyed listening to Jazz talk about the cubs. The passion in her voice when she spoke about them warmed my heart. She didn't realize it, but working with the cubs, seeing to their care and learning, was breaking down the walls she had erected one chunk at a time.

"Rook, where are you? Mack and I need to meet with you before dinner," Casey spoke through the Pride magic. I no longer needed the witches' magic to access both the Pack and Pride. Giving my loyalty to Casey before the challenge had solidified my connection. We had found a way to include me in both the Pack and Pride with Jerome's help.

"I'm at the meeting house, I'll be right up," I responded. Standing and stretching, I licked Jasmine's

hand and trotted off, stopping to shift back and don the clothes I had stashed at the gates before entering the Alpha's house to find Casey. She ran up to me as I closed the door, hugging me. I wrapped my arms around her and kissed the top of her head. "Hey there. Everything okay?" I inquired.

"Everything's fine, I just needed a hug from you. Come on, Mack's in the living room." She led the way and joined Mack, who was already reclining on one of the couches. "We have come up with a plan on how to get this Pride back in order."

I sat with them for the next two hours, listening and discussing their plans. I was so pleased with how Casey was taking charge, and their plan was unconventional, but I felt it would be beneficial in the end. It meant staying in South America longer than I had planned, part of that time spent away from the Pride and Jasmine. Still, I agreed it was necessary for re-establishing the South American Pride as a forward-thinking and progressive Pride. I leaned back when we had come to an agreement. "What about Jasmine?" I asked. It was the one question I hadn't brought up until this point.

Casey leaned forward. "That's a question I should be asking you, Rook. Is she the one? Is she your mate?"

"Yes, though she hasn't accepted that yet."

"Good." She settled back, snuggling under

Mack's arm and rubbing her belly. "She will continue her sessions with Katarina and her work with the cubs. Mack and I have already discussed putting a security detail on her while you are gone. You, of course, will get to choose who." Casey glanced at Mack before continuing, "She has a lot of things to work through, more than you can even imagine, and she needs to focus on healing herself before she can let anyone in, especially her mate. Don't give up on her, and be careful how far you try to push her right now. You will have to keep your cat on a short leash around her." Again she glanced at Mack. "But we both want you to know, we approve of your choice, and you have our blessing on your mating when she is ready."

I smiled even as my cat bristled at the words 'short leash'. "I want DJ to be her security," I blurted. "If I'm not available, he is my choice." I made a mental note to have a heart to heart with DJ before giving Jazz over to his protection. I knew he would take the job seriously and not let his emotions cloud his judgment. He would also be her shadow without Jazz ever knowing.

"Okay. Now that we have that decided, let's go eat. I'm starving." Casey stood.

"When aren't you hungry?" Mack laughed as he rose to join her.

She smacked his chest. "Hey now! I'm eating for two, or maybe even three," she teased him.

Mack's eyes followed her as she left the room, and he whispered, "Three?"

I clasped his shoulder. "Let's go, Dad, we can't keep her waiting."

"He's right. Let's go," Casey's voice echoed back to us.

We joined members of the Pride at the meeting house for dinner. Jonas was in the kitchen, helping Tamara. Those two were giving off enough sexual vibes to put everyone on edge. I peeked around the kitchen door to find Tamara trapped against the counter between Jonas's arms. "You both need to take that outside, to the jungle, far away. You have everyone on edge out here." I tried to make it a light joke, and Jonas growled at me. I knew then that his cat was in control and not Jonas. I walked over, keeping my voice low as I spoke, "Jonas, you need to get control before your cat takes her here in the kitchen with everyone listening." I clasped his shoulder, adding extra pressure to my grip. He growled again, not taking his eyes off Tamara.

I knew that this needed to end tonight, either with a mating or a final no from Tamara. I looked at her over Jonas's shoulder. "Tamara, it's time to make a decision. You see Jonas; his cat has more control than he does. You have to decide. Will you take him as your mate or not?" Her breath came in short spurts, her body vibrating. "Stop letting your fears choose. Reach down inside and let your instincts lead you. Mates are

152

destined and for life. Jonas has accepted it, will you?" I waited for her response.

"I'm scared, Rook," she whispered, her eyes never leaving Jonas.

"It's okay to be scared, but deep down, how do you feel?"

"It's him, it always has been." She exhaled.

Jonas moved at that instant, scooping her up and throwing her over his shoulder as he roared. He moved so fast after that, I didn't see him leave the building. I went out and joined Mack and Casey to finish dinner.

"Was that Jonas?" Casey asked.

"Yup."

"About damn time," Mack commented. "Maybe now, he can focus on more than convincing her."

"Hahaha. You know that won't happen. He'll be focused on showing her in every way, position, and place how much he loves her. We won't see them for a while." Casey smirked. "This is good for the Pride. The first mated couple since the fall of my father's reign. Now, maybe others will see that they can take the chance too."

We finished dinner with a happy and uplifting feel in the air. Pride members stopped by our table throughout the meal with well-wishes for the new Alpha and her pregnancy. With offers of help on one project or another, or simply to say hello and introduce themselves, the Pride members were finally seeing

Casey for the Alpha she was.

I took longer than usual to eat, hoping Jazz would join us for the meal, disappointed when she didn't show. Assuming she ate with the cubs, I finished and cleaned up after myself. Jasmine had experienced a very emotional day, I would give her time for now to recoup.

Seeing Katarina as I was leaving the dining area, I changed direction and headed toward her.

"Hello, Rook," she greeted me in her clipped, professional voice.

"Hello, Katarina," I replied gruffly. I still didn't care for her, but if she was what Jasmine needed to heal and move on, I would learn to accept her.

"Jasmine had a good session today." She peered up at me. "You were a part of that."

"I was?" I stood shocked. How was I a part of her session?

"Yes, she came to see me when you both returned to the village. Just being there for her today was the best thing you could have done. Now, I can't discuss what happened during our session, but I can let you know that patience, love, and support are what she needs for the time being. Keep it up." She lowered her eyes and returned to eating, effectively dismissing me. It should have pissed me off, but I was shocked that she had said something kind and encouraging.

I left her, my heart a bit lighter, and searched for

Rook

Jasmine. I wanted to see her again before I had to head out on my first mission for Casey.

Chapter 17

SIX months later

Rook

All I could think about as I traveled the rutted gravel-covered road to the village was taking a long hot shower and finding Jazz. This last mission had kept me away for over three weeks, and I was ready to be back. During the past four months, I had been on the road more than I had been home–if you could call the Pride village home. Being away from the Pack for over six months made me realize that was where I wanted to plant myself permanently. South America was way too hot and humid for my taste, and I was ready to go back—not without Jazz, though. Every time I returned from a mission, I saw her, and every time, she seemed to have blossomed more and more. Her daily sessions with Kat were helping her deal with her past, forgive herself, and realize she had a lot of life left to live. Her work with the cubs helped as well.

I pulled up outside the Alpha house and stepped out of the Jeep, finding Niko guarding the door today.

"Hey, Rook. Glad to have you back, man," he greeted me.

"Thanks, it feels good to be back." Part of taking on these missions was agreeing to step down as Casey's head of security. I handed that job over to Jonas and his elite guard. They had hand-picked a great group of shifters over the last six months and now had a strong security force devoted to Casey and the Pride. They had eradicated all the dangers and created the Pride they always wanted.

I turned to look down at the village, which was more of a tiny city now. New buildings had been erected for the Pride needs. A small hospital/doctor's office had been built with the latest technology that had been flown in so that all medical needs could be handled here instead of transported to Rio. Jax had done a fabulous job training the staff before he returned to the States. A schoolhouse and dormitory were positioned between the Alpha house and the center of town for the cubs and any on the way. Housing them on the third floor had been adequate for the first couple of months, but Casey decided they needed their own space. She had searched the globe for teachers and tutors to bring in, along with a child therapist who focused solely on our Pride. The cubs were out of school for the day and happily running around the center of town. It amazed me how resilient they were. They had done a complete one-eighty from when we had found them trapped in the basement, filthy and starving.

There were new houses built, a small store where Pride members could shop and request items not kept on hand. The newest addition that I saw was a small park with equipment for the kids to play on as well as areas for families to enjoy picnics or allow the cubs to romp around carefree.

I smiled, seeing all the changes that had come and also knowing the plans Casey and Mack had. I heard the creak of the front door opening behind me, and I turned in time to catch Jazz as she ran into my arms.

"I am so glad you're back." She sighed as she hugged me tightly. We had progressed to small touches and chaste kisses the last time I was home, but this display was new for me. I wrapped my arms around her, taking advantage of her sincere act to place a kiss on top of her head. I wanted to do much more but held myself and my cat in check. Plus, I was way too filthy to do much of anything.

"I'm glad to be back, sugar." I breathed in the

scent of her shampoo, a light coconut scent, and below that, I smelled the beginning of her arousal. My body responded in kind. "How have you been?" I asked as I moved her to my side, securing her under my arm as I strolled toward the house.

"I've been really good, other than missing you." She blushed. "Casey is probably tired of me asking her when you would get back." She laughed. I loved that sound, and my heart leapt when she turned that smile on me.

I don't know what happened in her sessions with Katarina, but I did notice the changes that came over Jasmine in the last six months. She smiled more, was more open with everyone, and had started responding to my small advances. Every time I returned, I made sure I searched her out, asked about what she did while I was gone, and showered her with affection. It was hard to hold myself back from what I really wanted to do. Right now, I wanted to throw her over my shoulder and take her in to shower with me. My hands itched to touch more than her shoulder or arms.

I wanted to taste her. Every. Damn. Inch. I wished to touch her and memorize her body, and then I dreamed of giving her pleasure she would never forget. I couldn't hold back much longer.

"Well, I'm back now, and in desperate need of a shower." I looked down at her. "Care to join me?" I waggled my eyebrows. I loved teasing her too, knowing she would say no.

"Maybe next time. You stink, and I wouldn't want to distract you from removing that stench." She giggled.

I stopped in my tracks, mouth hanging open as she continued to walk into the house. Did she just flirt with me? I shook my head no. I had to be hearing things. I glanced at Niko to see if he had heard her response.

"She's made some big strides while you were gone, boss." He grinned smugly. "You better catch up."

My cat roared inside at the expression on his face. I moved in the blink of an eye, standing nose to nose with him. "She. Is. Mine," I growled, causing Niko to put both hands up in surrender.

"We know, boss." His eyes went dark as he added, "But if you hurt her, you'll have the entirety of our security team on your ass." I nodded once in understanding. Niko backed up a step and smiled again. "Now, go get your girl, boss."

I took his advice and went inside the house in search of Jazz. I checked the rooms downstairs and didn't find her, so I ascended the stairs to the second floor. Mack and Casey had redone the master bedroom, thoroughly scrubbing any signs of Tomas away. Katarina was still in the far room in the right-wing. Jasmine had the bedroom closest to the stairs to the third floor. She chose that room when the cubs and harem were still living in the house and stayed there even after they moved out. Now, the third floor housed the elite guards on duty and myself. The rest of the rooms on the second floor were used as guest rooms.

I searched each one, except for Katarina's, and couldn't find her. Giving up for the moment, I climbed up to my room, preparing to shower and refresh myself. I'd search for Jazz once I was clean. When I looked around the common room, I noticed the door to my bedroom was open, and I heard water running. I moved through, excitement coursing through me. Maybe Jazz had changed her mind and decided to join me after all. I walked through the door to see her laying clothes out on my bed and unpacking the bag I thought I had left in the Jeep.

She glanced up and smiled. "I got the water running for you. I thought I would get your dirty laundry started and was just waiting to get the rest of your clothes." She looked me up and down, a hunger flashing in her eyes. "I also put fresh towels in the bathroom, three weeks is a long time to let linen sit. Just throw what you have on outside the door, and I'll get everything started."

I stared at her. Jazz was in my room, going through my bag, starting my shower, and offering to launder my clothes. All things a mate would do, and with a grin on her face. Not with her head down, not in

162

fear, but with a joyful smile on her face. I couldn't hold back. I marched over and framed her face with my hands placing a gentle kiss on her lips. "You don't have to do any of this for me, but I thank you for it." She stared into my eyes, not backing away. "We need to talk when I'm done. Will you come back and wait here for me?" I asked.

Jazz nodded yes. Then surprised me by rising to meet my lips again, her hands lightly grasping my shoulders as she hesitantly kissed me. I held still and let her explore, placing small kisses along my mouth. I vibrated with the need to take her kisses deeper but held back, letting her take the lead for now. She stepped back quickly, color climbing up her neck. She was gorgeous when she blushed, and I hoped to make her do it again soon. "I'll come back up after I get the wash started."

I blew out a breath and smiled. "Good." I went to the bathroom and quickly peeled off my clothes, wrapped a towel around my waist, opened the door, and held them out for her. The expression on her face satisfied my cat. She liked what she saw. I flexed a bit, my cat and I showing off for her. I placed my clothes on the chair outside the door. "I'll just leave these here for you, I hate to waste hot water." I turned around and closed the door partially, dropping the towel as I did so, giving Jazz a good view of my ass. I heard the hiss of her intake of breathy, and my body stirred at the sound, hardening like a rock.

Jumping into the shower, I scrubbed off the weeks of dirt and sweat, itching to relieve the pressure that had built up, but I wouldn't. Relief would come with Jazz beneath me…or next to me…or against a wall…or even in this very shower. Soon.

Chapter 18

Jazz

Holy hell, what had I just done? I rushed downstairs with Rook's clothes to get them started. I had kissed him, but he kissed me first, so that was okay, right? But then, he came out with only a towel on, and my heart stopped. He was the most beautiful man I had ever seen. His body was chiseled with muscles that were used and not created simply for show. His tattoos fascinated me, covering his upper arms, part of his back, and down his abdomen. I had wanted to reach out and trace every single one, first with my fingers and then with my mouth. But then he turned around and dropped his towel altogether, and my knees almost gave way. I started tingling in places I never thought I would.

On the way back from the laundry, I ran to

Katarina's room. I didn't know if she had a session right now, but I tried anyway. I pounded on her door. "Kat, are you in there? I need to talk to you!" I slammed my fist again, and Kat opened her door. She looked as if she had just gotten out of bed, hair messy and belting a robe around her waist quickly.

"What is it, Jasmine?" she asked, her eyes checking to make sure I wasn't injured.

"It's Rook. Can you talk?" I gasped. My body was still on overdrive, and I didn't know how to handle it.

Kat glanced over her shoulder and opened the door, fully allowing me in. "What happened with Rook?"

"He kissed me."

"How did that make you feel?" she asked.

"Stop with the therapist crap. You have helped me come so far, to forgive myself, to realize that what happened to me wasn't my fault and that it's okay for me to want someone in my life, to want a mate. But I've never had anything like this. Felt like this. What do I do?" I whined.

Kat smiled at me. "Jasmine, do you trust Rook?"

"Yes, with my life."

"Does he seem to have the same feelings?"

"I think so." I bit my fingernail. "No, I know he does."

Rook

Kat sighed. "Then it sounds like you should give in and see where your feelings take you. You trust Rook, and you know Casey trusts him, therefore, give him a chance. You may find that your mate has been right in front of you. I think you're ready. Enjoy it, Jasmine." Kat hugged me.

I took a few deep breaths. "Okay." Kat led me to her door and ushered me out, closing it in my face. *You can do this, Jasmine. You're ready for the next step.* I bolstered my confidence and headed back to Rook's room. There was no reason to fear him. I trusted him and knew he would never hurt me. My sessions with Kat had really helped me face my fears, forgive myself and those who had hurt me. Forgiveness was a huge factor in my healing process, but I was ready to take the next step, to allow myself to feel again, and to let my instincts take over. My cat purred inside me in agreement. She was ready to go and pounce on Rook herself.

Scared and giddy at the same time, I laughed on the way up the stairs. My body warmed at the thought of Rook, naked and wet. Visions of surprising him in the shower filled my head as I rushed into the room. I wasn't that bold in real life yet, but in my imagination, I did that and more.

I had myself so worked up, I didn't hear him come out of the bathroom. The sound of him clearing his throat brought me out of my daydream. I looked up to see him standing in the doorway, a towel slung low on his hips, and water still beading on his chest. My mouth went dry, and my girlie bits went into overdrive at the sight.

With a mischievous glint in his eye, he grasped the end of the towel. "Like what you see, do you?"

My gaze followed his hand, words escaping me. My breath came in shallow gasps as I waited to see what he would do with that towel. My eyes followed him as he made his way to the bed where his clean clothes lay, and his deep chuckle broke my trance. "No...uh, yes...I was just waiting...like you asked." My words stumbled out of my mouth, falling over each other.

He turned away from me and dropped his towel, flexing as he reached for his boxers. I watched as he donned them and his jeans, forgoing the T-shirt before turning to face me. With a smile, he sat and scooted back against the headboard.

Patting the bed next to him, he invited me to join him. "Come, talk to me. I've missed seeing your smile."

I shook my head. "I don't know if that's a good idea."

He held up his hands. "I only want to talk." That grin crept across his face again. "Unless you had other ideas."

"No," I sputtered. "Talking is fine." I blushed,

feeling the heat rise up my neck. I knew I must be a pretty shade of red by now. After searching his face, and against my better judgment, I did as he asked. Instead of directly next to him, I sat in front of him, one leg crooked underneath me so I could see his face, and well, all of him while we talked. "I've missed you too," I said. "Will you be leaving again?"

"No, that was my last mission for Casey. I'm done, and back for good," he replied, gently resting his hand on my knee. He looked away lost in thought, and his thumb absently rubbed circles on my thigh. He glanced back at me. "What have you been doing while I was away?'

"Not much. We moved the cubs and the tutors into the dormitories and finally have them on a set school schedule." I smiled. "The rest of the harem have also moved out of the house and into their own place. They aren't ready to be alone yet, but they are doing much better. They started a garden for Tamara and enjoy working in it. It gives them something to do where they don't have to interact much with the rest of the Pride." I took a breath. "Jonas and Niko are the only men they truly trust right now, besides Mack. So, those two check on them throughout the day. Jonas still posts guards at night to make them feel safe." I babbled on about what had changed in the Pride over the last three weeks as he watched, encouraging me to continue with his handing on my leg. It was hard to focus when he touched me. Having his heat so close, made me want to curl up with him and soak it in. I avoided talking about myself, choosing to focus on the cubs, and especially the bond Marla had with two of them.

Rook laughed. "Sounds like she is smitten. I wonder how Sterling will take it."

"I don't know, but she is already talking about taking them back to the States with her. I think it would be a good idea. She is good for them, considering she is the same species as the little girl." I smiled.

"What about the boy?" Rook asked.

"He's a fox. He is the only cub that wasn't fathered by Tomas. He found him wandering the jungle on his last outing and brought him home. We have searched the outlying areas in hopes of locating his family but have had no luck."

Rook nodded. "The Pack may be the best choice for him. Sterling is actually a silver fox. Having another of the same or similar species would help the cub." He laughed. "I can't wait to see how that goes down!" His eyes met mine then, and he opened his arms. "Come here. We've talked about everything else, but now I want to talk about you. Will you join me? I want to hold you."

I hesitated. My cat didn't.

Chapter 19

Rook

𝒯 held my breath as I waited for her to decide if she would join me or not. I knew I took a risk asking her, but lying here with her so close was killing me, and my cat was demanding more physical contact than the simple touch of my hand. I watched the emotions cross her face as she decided. Trusting a man enough to freely lay with him, even with our clothes on, was a big step for her. This would show me how far she had come in the last six months of therapy. Our kiss earlier was a good indication, but I wanted to see if that was just a one-time occurrence or if Jasmine was really ready to take what we had to the next, or even the furthest, level. I knew I was.

With my missions for Casey done, I knew I

would be heading back to the States and the Pack soon. I wanted to take Jasmine with me. I wished to show her what a true and loving Pack looked like and how we worked together. The Pride was doing well, but it would be a long time before they were at the level of the Black Mountain Pack. I didn't want her to have to wait that long to find out. I had already spoken to Mack and Casey, and they said it was up to Jasmine. If she chose to go with me, it would be with their blessing.

She blew out a breath. "Okay."

I waited as she crawled up and lay next to me, putting her head on my chest before I wrapped my arms around her. I kissed the top of her head as my cat and I sighed together, finally happy and content. "Thank you." I rubbed my hand up and down her back, comforting both her and me. "Now, tell me how things are with you. I truly want to know, and so does my cat." I lay there, holding her and waiting. I'd wait all night if I had to. I wouldn't let her go until she shared with me.

It took her a few minutes, but she softly replied, "I'm better." She turned her face up to look at me. "I'm not one hundred percent, but I'm a lot better." She beamed.

I took the chance and leaned down to brush a kiss across her lips. I took it as a positive sign when she didn't tense up or back away. "I'm glad. Is there anything I can do to help?"

"Be patient with me." She lay her head back

down. "This is good, just holding me is good. My cat likes it, too. Kat has helped me through our therapy sessions, but she said it's time to start taking chances again, to let my cat take the lead, and let instinct fall back into place. Whatever that means," she huffed. "Right now, she and I both want to lay here with you, if that's okay," she whispered.

"Of course." I smiled, but she couldn't see me. "Are you hungry?" I asked.

"A little."

"I'll have something delivered here. Then we can eat and relax. Sound good?"

"Yeah." She sighed, her body relaxing even more into mine.

The feel of her along my chest and thigh were making it difficult to take things slow. My body hardened further with every breath she took. Those breaths brought her covered breasts against my bare chest. I wanted to remove her shirt and bra so that we were bare together. I growled low in my chest as I reined that thought in and contacted Tamara through the Pride. *"Tam, can you have someone put together two meals and bring them to the Alpha house for Jazz and me?"*

"Of course, Rook." I heard the excitement in her response. *"Is everything okay?"*

"Yes, Tam. Everything is perfect." I broke the connection and settled in, Jasmine wrapped in my arms,

to wait for the food to arrive.

As usual, Tamara outdid herself when she sent the tray. Jonas was a lucky man with a woman who could cook that well. The way the pheromones radiated off those two, the mating may have happened months ago, but Jonas' cat still had days where it decided that everyone Tamara came into contact with was a threat. I knew the feeling, mine was becoming the same way as well. I needed to take it slow with Jazz, but my cat was beginning not to care. The physical contact today wasn't helping to keep him in check.

I watched Jazz devour her portion of the food from the tray, and once we were both sated, we settled back against the headboard. I sat up a bit more than before because it was time to have a serious discussion. I reached down, entwining my fingers with hers, and brought her hand to my mouth to kiss each of her fingers. "Jasmine, I need to talk to you. I know you have been through more than I can imagine, and you have taken huge strides to heal with Kat…" I paused, taking a deep breath. It was all or nothing now. "I am so proud of how far you have come, but I can't hold back what I feel anymore. From the moment I met you, my cat and I both knew you were destined to be ours. Our mate. I also knew you weren't ready for that. But now that I have completed my missions for Casey, I'm no longer needed. I'll be heading back to the States to join Jerome and my Pack."

Rook

I scanned her face and held my breath, waiting for her reaction. If she denied me, I knew I wouldn't search out anyone. It was her or nothing. I squeezed her hand in comfort and encouragement, although it was more for me than her. I took it as a positive sign when she squeezed back and smiled.

"When would you leave?" she whispered.

"As soon as I can report to Mack and Casey about this last mission and get my things in order. Jerome has already contacted me to request my ETA. I have to let him know within the next day or two." I reached over and caressed her chin, raising her eyes to meet mine. "I'd like you to go with me." Her eyes grew big and shiny with unshed tears.

"Really?" She grinned bigger.

"If you want to, yes. It would make me the happiest man around." I kissed her forehead. What I really wanted to do was take her lips and show her how much I desired her. I had to tread lightly; I could let the passion go when she said yes.

She looked down at our clasped hands, running her fingers over our joined hands and looked back up at me. "I want to be with you." She took a deep breath. "Wherever you are, I want to be with you, but I'm scared."

"That's okay, it's normal to be scared, but you don't have to be because I'll be with you. I think you'll like the Pack. We will stay with Jerome and Susan until my house is ready. I am sure it needs a good cleaning, and it's fairly empty since I'm the only one who has ever lived there. You can fill it up and make it yours, too. You will love Susan, and I know she will love you." I pulled her close, releasing her hand to frame her face. I scanned her eyes and found acceptance before I leaned in for a kiss. It started off sweet, but when she opened for me, the pent up need took over, and when she reacted without hesitation, I let my feelings pour through.

I felt Mack in my mind, and I knew he wanted to talk, but now was not the time. I shut down all connections to focus on Jasmine and the pleasure I planned to bring her. I took my time kissing her, showing her with each stroke of my tongue everything I wished to do with her. My cat and I both agreed she had too many clothes on. I released her lips and trailed kisses down her neck, listening to her breathing and soft moans for any sign of hesitation on her part. Hearing her little mewls of pleasure spurred me on. I grasped the hem of her shirt and began raising it. Leaning back, I made eye contact. "Okay?" I rasped out. If anything scared her, I would stop, it would be hard, but for her, I'd do anything. Her breath came in short gasps as she nodded. "I need you to say it, Jasmine. If anything scares you, I'll stop, but I need you to vocalize it."

"Yes, don't stop." Her voice was deep with need.

Rook

I pulled her shirt up and off, throwing it to the side and simply looked at her. She was splendid with her breasts barely contained by her bra, and just below that were three scars. She covered them, lowering her eyes. I moved her hand. "There isn't anything you need to hide from me. I want to see all of you." I leaned forward and kissed each scar as she lay back. I kissed between her breasts, up her neck, and captured her lips again, giving her time to adjust to having my hands and mouth on her. My erection pressed against the zipper of my jeans, and I was glad I had chosen to don my boxers, or else I would have been in pain.

I took my time tracing my fingers along her skin, peppering her with kisses along the way. She had relaxed fully and was writhing beneath me.

"More, Rook, I need more."

I smiled because she spoke, telling me what she desired. Her nipples were hard beneath her bra, and I licked one through the fabric before sucking it into my mouth. Her back arched off the bed at the contact, and she moaned. I took the opportunity to reach behind her to unclasp the fabric. Releasing her nipple with a pop, I swept the bra away. I took a breast in each hand, weighing them, rolling her nipples in my fingers, watching her emotions play out on her face. Her eyes were still closed as she bit her bottom lip. A sure sign she was enjoying this as much as I was. I leaned forward, giving each nipple equal attention, laving and

177

sucking them into even harder peaks. As my mouth focused on her breasts, my hand roamed over her body, running along her jeans, up her inner thighs, almost to her apex but skipping over it to touch the skin along her waistband.

She huffed out a breath when I passed over her womanhood. I left her breasts and kissed a trail down to her waist, unbuttoning her jeans as I did. Glancing up at her, I noticed her watching me, and I hesitated a moment. However, when she lifted her hips, I took that as my sign to divest her of the rest of her clothing. I dragged her underwear down with her jeans and tossed them to join her shirt and bra on the side of the bed. I could smell she how wet and ready she was, her sweet and musky scent tantalizing my nose.

I licked just above her curls and inhaled deeply, letting out a low snarl. My cat was demanding I mark her right there, but I held him back. There would be time for the mate's mark. Right now, this was about Jasmine and showing her there was more to loving. It would be more than sex…this time. I lowered past the apex of her legs and kissed each thigh, slightly nipping at her skin, and running my tongue along the sting to soothe it.

She gasped, and her legs fell open for me, showing me her center, her curls glistening with her nectar, her body begging me for more. Reaching down, she ran a hand through my hair, and I took the first taste of the last woman I would ever want to be with. Her flavor burst inside my mouth as I brought her to the edge and let her fall. I sat back, licking my lips, and my cat swelled with pride, knowing we brought our mate to the first of many climaxes.

I kissed up her body, taking her mouth in mine and sharing her taste with her. She wrapped her arms around me, her fingernails grazing down my back. I stared down at her, at the pleasure radiating from her face.

"Rook, I need more. I need you."

"Are you sure?" I knew I had given her pleasure, but I still wanted to make sure she was ready. Now was not the time to jeopardize this mating.

She pushed at my waistband. "Yes, I want you. Inside."

I stripped my jeans and boxers off, my erection springing forth and settling back between her legs. Jasmine grasped my face and brought it down for a kiss. Her eyes opened to meet mine, flashing to feline and back as I entered her. I held still, allowing her body adjust to me. A feeling washed over me that I couldn't explain--a connection clicked in my mind as my heart settled and filled with her. My cat roared inside with satisfaction, urging me to complete the mating by marking her. My eyes shifted to the spot where her neck and shoulder met. The place that would bear my mark. I held my cat in check. I wouldn't do that until she was ready. Meeting her eyes again, I began to move and watched her pupils dilate with the same need overwhelming me.

I had held off taking her for so long I knew I wouldn't last long. I wanted to draw this out for her as much as possible, but she spurred me on. Wrapping her legs around my waist and holding me tighter. She pulled my head to her neck and whispered, "Make me yours completely, Rook. Mark me."

My cat and I joined at that moment, and with one final thrust, I felt Jasmine's orgasm take over, and I released mine, my teeth elongating and biting into that sweet spot that would carry my mark for the rest of our lives. Jazz screamed out her orgasm, and I licked the wound to help hasten the healing.

I rolled to the side, bringing her with me. Now that the passion had subsided, I was worried she would regret what we had done. I never intended to mark her the first time we made love. I rubbed her back as she nuzzled against me and waited for her reaction.

"Are you okay?" I whispered.

She gazed up and smiled. "I'm perfect." She ran her fingers through the light dusting of hair on my chest. "I never knew how good it could be, and now I feel…" she hesitated. "I feel whole as if a missing part of me is home."

"Me too, darling." My body relaxed, and we drifted off. I should get cleaned up, but I didn't care at this moment. I had my mate asleep in my arms where she belonged.

Chapter 20

Jasmine

$\mathcal{I}$ woke still wrapped in Rook's arms and laid there, listening to his breathing as he slept. I felt like I was in a dream. I hadn't expected to fall into his arms so quickly or easily, but he was so attentive, and I never experienced the fear with him that used to come with the thought of intimacy with anyone else. Kat told me during our sessions that I should trust my cat and her instincts, and that was exactly what I had done. When he bit down to mark me, the final cage I had kept my cat in blew away. I no longer had walls or boxes holding things back in my mind. I felt happy and complete. I also felt like I wanted to run for a very long time. My cat was stretching in my mind, preparing.

Rook stirred as we lay there, realizing I was

awake.

"Hey there," I whispered.

"Hey," he responded in a raspy voice. "How are you doing?" Concern was etched on his face.

"I'm great." I smiled and hesitated to say anything else.

"But..." he coaxed.

"I want to run," I blurted out, blushing. I had never been forward, but with Rook, I felt like I could say anything. That would take some getting used to. I knew from our connection that he wouldn't judge me. I also felt his cat through the bond, flirting with mine, and my body started tingling. I wanted another romp with them both.

"Then let's go run." His eyes twinkled as he got up and walked to the door, stark naked.

"Shouldn't we get dressed?" I asked, pulling the sheet up to my chest.

"There's no one in the house right now. We can go down the back stairs and shift outside. I don't want to go far on your first run. Come on." He winked and walked out the door.

With trepidation, I climbed out of bed and followed him, tiptoeing out the door and searching for anyone who might still be in the house. I found him at the top of the back stairs smiling. When he saw I followed, he descended. I had two choices, to follow him or turn around and get dressed. I took a deep breath and ran to the stairs. The door was standing open when I descended, and through it sat Rook in all his tiger glory. He swished his tail, waiting for me.

"I haven't shifted in years, Rook. I don't know how long it will take."

"Just let her take over. She knows what to do, don't fight her." He spoke through our bond. I closed my eyes and opened myself to her. I could feel her excitement, and within moments, the change was done. I stretched my muscles, remembering how it felt to be in this body. My white fur gleamed in the sunlight, and Rook rubbed against me, talking to me through our bond again, *"Let me know when you are ready. Mack wants to see us before we take off if that's okay with you. He is out front with Casey, Jonas, and Tamara."*

My cat wanted to see them; she wanted to show off to everyone. She was one of the reasons I had become such a favorite among Tomas' friends. I was a rare white tiger, and the rarer the shifter, the higher the demand. But that was in my past, and Rook hadn't chosen me because of that. This was the first time he was seeing my tiger. He wanted me for me. Our shifters had been destined since birth. I took a moment to thank the gods that he had been brought back to the Pride, that he had been a part of Tomas' demise, and that I had taken the leap to trust him last night. *"Okay, let's go see them."*

He led the way around front where they waited.

Casey gasped when I emerged behind Rook. Tamara oohed, and the men stared.

"Jasmine, you are beautiful," Casey said. "Welcome to the family." She knelt down, as best as her bulging belly would allow, and opened her arms. I went over and let her hug my neck as I sniffed her hair, her belly resting against my chest. Her cubs chose that moment to kick pretty darn hard. I chuffed as she laughed, reaching for Mack to help her up. "I think they like you, too."

"I am glad to see you two have completed the mating." Mack chuckled and glanced at me, running his hand over my fur. "I wasn't sure how much longer Rook was going to be able to hold out. This is a good sign for the Pride as well. Even though I assume you will be returning to the Pack with him, you give the rest of the Pride members hope of finding their mates as well. Welcome, Jasmine. Know that we will always be here for you, even if you are a continent away." Mack turned to Rook. "Have fun running, but don't stay too long. I just heard from Da, and he needs you back as soon as you both can travel." Rook nodded his tiger head at him.

Tamara stepped forward then. "Jasmine, all arrangements for the cubs are complete. The last of the tutors arrived today, and everyone is getting along famously. Marla has decided to take the two that have bonded with her back to the States and plans to travel with you both when you go." A tear slipped down her face. "It won't be the same without you, but I am so happy that you found your mate." Tamara looked over her shoulder at Jonas. "I only hope the rest of the women can find theirs." Jonas wrapped an arm around her shoulders, and Tamara grasped his hand. "I also wanted to let you know that I have accepted Jonas as my mate. We haven't finished the ritual, obviously, but I finally stopped being scared and took the leap. Seeing how far you have come with Kat's help made me realize I didn't want to waste any more time giving him the runaround. We are holding a celebration tonight and hope you and Rook can stay long enough to attend." She wiped the tears that continued to escape.

I rubbed against her leg and flicked my tail at her, hoping she would take that as the yes I meant it as.

"If we want to have time to get ready for the celebration, we need to go now for that run," Rook spoke and led me into the brush just past Mack and Casey. We ran from there.

For the next two hours, we ran and frolicked. Chasing small game, rolling, and playing like we were cubs again, only returning once exhaustion threatened to overtake me. We entered through the back door and didn't shift back until we were in Rook's room again. We were both sweaty and dirty and in need of a shower. Rook came up and wrapped his arms around my waist. "We could conserve water by showering together."

I ran my hands up his arms and encircled his neck. Standing on tiptoe, I kissed his neck and replied, "Sounds like a good plan to me." He swept me off my feet and carried me into the bathroom, closing the door with his foot. The great thing about the Alpha house is each bathroom had its own water heater, so we didn't have to wait for the water to heat up. Rook joined me under the spray. We eventually got around to getting clean after a few rounds of other things.

We joined the rest of the Pride at the meeting house to celebrate Jonas and Tamara. It was good to see the Pride celebrating something. Everyone was happy, and the layer of evil that used to hang over the Pride was gone. Mack and Casey were turning things around.

I found Marla among the crowd looking worried. "What's wrong, Marla?"

"I hate to leave the cubs. I know they are safe, but I'm ready to get them on the plane and headed back home with me." She gazing at me. "You are good for him, you know." She smiled. "I'm glad you decided to accept him and come back with us. You'll love the Pack." She took my hand and squeezed it, glancing toward the dormitory.

"Go check on them. No one will miss you. Make sure they have everything they need packed." I let go of her hand as she walked off. I joined Rook at the Alpha's table. I could read the exhaustion on his face, but a slight gasp from Casey took my attention away from him. "Casey, are you okay?"

She waved off my concern. "Yes, the cubs are overly active tonight. Why don't you take Rook and make sure you have everything you need. Niko is ready to take you to the plane when you and Marla are ready." She smiled through another rough kick from the cubs.

"Okay, I know Marla is ready to go." I leaned over and hugged her. "You need to rest, too. Those cubs will be here any day. I hate that I'll miss it, but you are in good hands with Tamara. Let us know the moment they arrive."

Mack stood and embraced me, placing a kiss on my head. He leaned down and whispered in my ear, "You take care of him now. If you don't, I'll hunt you down myself." He patted my shoulder and smiled.

Rook stood and reached for me as we gathered our things from the house. Niko had Marla and two very sleepy cubs already in the Jeep. Our bags were thrown in the back, and we climbed in. It was an uncomfortable fit, my hips were jammed between the metal door and the bony elbow of a cub. Jeeps weren't meant to hold four adult shifters and two cubs, but we would make do. The drive would take about an hour to the landing strip, where one of Jerome's jets waited for us.

We unfolded ourselves and fell out of the Jeep when we arrived. Niko unloaded all the luggage onto the plane while Marla got the cubs onboard. Rook and I were the last to board. The opulence of the interior was unexpected, but my hips thanked me when I snuggled into a plush seat and buckled in with Rook sitting next to me and pulling me into his side before covering us both with a blanket.

The pilot took off without a bump or rattle. Rook twined his fingers with mine as we flew into the air. "Sleep Jazz, I've got you."

Closing my eyes, I drifted off, dreaming of the cubs we might someday have.

About the Author

Mother to two boys, 3 four-legged babies, and wife to a loving husband who doesn't mind the extra voices in her head Miranda grew up on a dairy farm in Illinois, but calls Portland, TN home now. She is an avid reader, coffee addict, and loves her day job. Though her true passion is in creating her own worlds, characters, and stories for her readers.

Website: www.mirandalynn.com
Facebook www.facebook.com/MirandaLyn
Twitter: @MirandaLynnBks
Email: mirandalynnbooks@gmail.com

Other Books By Miranda Lynn

Destiny Finds Her Blair's Destiny
Black Mountain Series Mack Rook Sterling

61590336R00113